Hall Caine

A Son of Hagar

Vol. I

Hall Caine

A Son of Hagar
Vol. I

ISBN/EAN: 9783337020644

Printed in Europe, USA, Canada, Australia, Japan

Cover: Foto ©Andreas Hilbeck / pixelio.de

More available books at **www.hansebooks.com**

. . . Mr. Caine's calm and spiritual writings will for them be always a sealed book, only to be admired when it has become the fashion to do so. . . . Poor Sim, who undergoes the long martyrdom of unfounded suspicion, is one of the best conceived characters we have met with in modern fiction. If we ventured on comparisons, we might seem to praise it too highly.'—*Academy.*

'If this book, as we believe to be the case, is Mr. Caine's first essay as a novelist, it must be at once conceded that it is a most successful one, so successful that its pages remind the reader of some of the best attributes of Charles Reade. The story has almost all the vigour of the author of "The Cloister and the Hearth," with almost more than that writer's picturesqueness as a romancist. . . . Poor weak-kneed, but true-souled, Simeon Stagg is a masterpiece of character-drawing. His contrition for a crime which he had not committed, and his acceptance of the "position of a guilty man from whose contaminating touch all other men might fairly shrink," is described with a pathetic power which would alone go far to place Mr. Caine in the foremost file of romancists.'—*Standard.*

'A very noble note is struck in "The Shadow of a Crime," by Hall Caine. . . . The novel is one which it does the author great honour to have written, and which it should do a reader appreciable good to read. . . . It is very seldom indeed that there appears a novel so fine in conception, so heroic in tone, so healthy in its associations, so attractive, and so natural in its descriptions; so altogether good, sound and improving.'—*Illustrated London News.*

'One of the most powerful novels which we have seen for a long time past is Mr. Hall Caine's "The Shadow of a Crime." . . . The plot is worked out with singular power. . . Few more powerful scenes are to be found in any novel. The reader will not fail to learn to love some of the characters, even though he should learn to despise others. But he will find from the first of the story to the end of it there are vigour and attractiveness, and his interest will never for a moment be lessened.'—*Scotsman.*

'We should describe the novel as powerful in detail.'—*Times.*

'Mr. Hall Caine has some of George Eliot's power of indicating rustic character by a few touches.'—*Spectator.*

'Moving and powerful; takes hold of the imagination.'—*Daily News.*

'It must be a relief to readers and reviewers alike to come across such a fresh and stirring series of narratives as Mr. Caine presents in this Cumberland story. . . We have to thank Mr. Caine for a fresh, picturesque, and thoroughly original story, which will, no doubt, be one of the books of the season, and the success of which may well induce the author to prosecute his new career.'—*Liverpool Mercury.*

'We have no hesitation in saying that this is one of the most remarkable books that has been published in the last quarter of this century. . . . . One of the most unique of modern literary efforts.'—*Whitehall Review.*

'Mr. Hall Caine is emphatically a new novel-writer, and "The Shadow of a Crime" introduces a fresh individuality into the library of romances of the time. . . . Mr. Caine shows the hand of a master. . . . The novel is high-class work, at the same time that it is full of keen interest for the ordinary novel-reader.'—*School Board Chronicle.*

'Full of human nature.'—*Pall Mall Gazette.*

'Mr. Hall Caine will win a foremost place among novelists of the century.'—*Figaro.*

'At a bound he has taken rank among the first of our novelists.'—*Western Morning News.*

CHATTO & WINDUS, PICCADILLY, W.

A SON OF HAGAR

A Romance of our Time

By HALL CAINE

God hath heard the voice of the lad where he is'

IN THREE VOLUMES
VOL. I

London
CHATTO AND WINDUS, PICCADILLY
1887

R. D. BLACKMORE.

' *It must be an exceeding great reward, beyond all the rewards of material success, to know that you have written a book that is deep, tranquil, strong and pure. You have nobly earned that knowledge. Across the more than thirty years that divide us, the elder from the younger brother, the veteran from the raw comrade, the coming from the departing generation, let me offer my hand to you as to a master of our craft.*

To the author, then, of a romance that has no equal save in Scott, I humbly dedicate this romance of mine.

H. C.

barn = child ; dusta = dost thou ; hasta = hast thou.

laal = little ; leet = alight ; girt = great.

sista = seëst thou.

varra = very.

wadsta = wouldst thou.

wilta = wilt thou.

Shaf ! = *an expression of contempt.*

PREFACE.

In my first novel, 'The Shadow of a Crime,' I tried to penetrate into the soul of a brave, unselfish, long-suffering man, and to lay bare the processes by which he raised himself to a great height of self-sacrifice. In this novel the aim has been to penetrate into the soul of a bad man, and to lay bare the processes by which he is tempted to his fall. To find a character that shall be above all common tendencies to guilt and yet tainted with the plague-spot of evil hidden somewhere; then to watch the first sharp struggle of what is good in the man with what is bad, until he is in the coil of his temptation; and finally, to show in what tragic ruin a man of strong passions, great will and power of mind may resist the force that precipitates him and save his soul alive — this is, I trust, a motive no less worthy, no less profitable to study, in the utmost result no less heroic and inspiring, than that of tracing the upward path of noble types of mind. For me there has been a pathetic, and I think purifying interest in looking into the soul of this man and seeing it corrode beneath the touch of a powerful temptation until at the last, when it seems to lie spent, it rises again in strength and shows that the human heart has no depths in which it is lost. If this character had been equal to my intention, it might have been a real contribution to fiction, and far as I know it to fall short of the first deep glow of feeling in which it was conceived, it is, I think, new to the novel, though it holds a notable

place in the drama — it would be pre-
sumptuous to say where — unnecessary,
also, as I have made no disguise of my
purpose.

One of the usual disadvantages of choosing
a leading character that is off the lines of
heroic portraiture is that the author may
seem to be in sympathy with a base part
in life and with base opinions. In this
novel I run a different risk. I shall not
be surprised if I provoke some hostility
in making the bad man justify his
course by the gaunt and grim morality
that masquerades as the morality of our own
time, while the good man is made to justify
his one dubious act by the full and sincere
and just morality that too often wears now
the garb of vice—the morality of the books
of Moses. This novel relies, I trust, on the
sheer humanities alone, but among its less
aggressive purposes is that of a plea for

the natural rights of the bastard. Those rights have been recognised in every country and by every race, except one, since the day when the outcast woman in the wilderness hearkened to the cry from heaven which said, 'God hath heard the voice of the lad, where he is.' In England alone have the rights of blood been as nothing compared with the rights of property, and it is part of the business of this novel to exhibit these interests at a climax of strife. I have no fear that any true-hearted person will accuse me of a desire to cast reproach upon marriage as an ordinance. Recognising the beauty and the sanctity of marriage, I have tried to show that true marriage is a higher thing than a ceremony, and that the people who use the gibbet and stake for offenders against its forms are too often those who see no offence in the violation of its spirit.

My principal scenes are again among the mountains of Cumberland; but in this second attempt I have tried to realize more completely their solitude and sweetness, their breezy healthfulness, and their scent as of new-cut turf, by putting them side by side with scenes full of the garrulous clangour and the mal-odour of the dark side of London.

When I began, I thought to enlarge the popular knowledge of our robust north-country by the addition of some whimsical character and quaint folk-lore. If much of this quiet local atmosphere has had to make way before one strong current of tragic feeling, I trust some of it remains that is fresh and bracing in the incidents of the booth, the smithy, the dalesman's wedding, the rushbearing, the cockfighting and the sheep-shearing. Those readers of the earlier book who found human nature and an

element of humour in the *patois* will regret
with me the necessity so to modify the
dialect in this book as to remove from it
nearly all the racy quality that comes of
intonation.

I ought to add that one of my characters,
Parson Christian, is a portrait of a dear,
simple, honest soul long gone to his account,
and that the words here put into his mouth
are oftener his own than mine.

I trust this book may help to correct a
prevailing misconception as to the morals
and mind of the typical English peasantry.
It is certain that the conventional peasant
of literature, the broad-mouthed rustic in
a smock-frock, dull-eyed, mulish, beetle-
headed, doddering, too vacant to be vicious,
too doltish to do amiss, does not exist as a
type in England. What does exist in every
corner of the country is a peasantry speaking a *patois* that is often of varying

inflections but is always full of racy poetry, illiterate and yet possessed of a vast oral literature, sharing brains with other classes more equally than education, humorous, nimble-witted, clear-sighted, astute, cynical, not too virtuous, and having a lofty contempt for the wiseacres of the town.

The manners and customs, the folk-lore and folk-talk of Cumberland are far from exhausted in my two Cumberland novels; but it is not probable that I will work in this vein again. In parting from it, may I venture to hope that here and there a reader grown tired of the life of the great cities has sometimes found it a relief to escape with me into these mountain solitudes and look upon a life as real and more true; a life that is humble and yet not low; a life in which men may be men, and the rude people of the soil need study the face of no master save nature alone?

H. C.

CONTENTS.

A SON OF HAGAR.

BOOK THE FIRST.

RETRO ME, SATHANA.

VOL. I.   1

PROLOGUE.

I<small>T</small> was a chill December morning. The atmosphere was dense with fog in the dusky chamber of a London police-court; the lights were bleared and the voices drowsed. A woman carrying a child in her arms had been half dragged, half pushed into the dock. She was young; beneath her dishevelled hair her face showed almost girlish. Her features were pinched with pain; her eyes had at one moment a serene look, and at the next moment a look of wild defiance. Her dress had been rich; it was now torn and damp, and clung in dank folds to her

1—2

limbs.   The child she carried appeared to
be four months old.   She held it con-
vulsively at her breast, and when it gave
forth a feeble cry she rocked it mechanic-
ally.

'Your worship, I picked this person out
of the river at ha'-past one o'clock this
morning,' said a constable.   'She had
throwed herself off the steps of Blackfriars
Bridge.'

'Had she the child with her?' asked the
bench.

'Yes, your worship; and when I brought
her to land I couldn't get the little one out
of her arms nohow—she clung that tight
to it.   The mother, she was insensible:
but the child, it opened its little eyes and
cried.'

'Have you not learned her name?'

'No, sir; she won't give us no answer
when we ask her that.'

'I am informed,' said the clerk, 'that

against all inquiries touching her name and circumstances she keeps a rigid silence. The doctor is of opinion, your worship, that the woman is not entirely responsible.'

'Her appearance in court might certainly justify that conclusion,' said the magistrate.

The young woman had gazed vacantly about her with an air of indifference. She seemed scarcely to realize that through the yellow vagueness the eyes of a hundred persons were centred on her haggard face.

'Anybody here who knows her?' asked the bench.

'Yes, your worship; I found out the old woman alonger she lodged.'

'Let us hear the old person.'

A woman in middle life—a little, confused, aimless, uncomfortable body—stepped into the box. She answered to the name of Drayton. Her husband was an hotel porter.

She had a house in Pimlico. A month ago one of her rooms on the first-floor back had been to let. She put a card in her window, and the prisoner applied. Accepted the young lady as tenant, and had been duly paid her rent. Knew nothing of who she was or where she came from. Couldn't even get her name. Had heard her call the baby Paul. That was all she knew.

'Her occupation, my good woman, what was it ?'

'Nothing ; she hadn't no occupation, your worship.'

'Never went out ? Not at night ?'

'No, sir ; leastways not at night, sir. I hopes your worship takes me for an honest woman, sir.'

'Did nothing for a living, and yet she paid you. Did you board her ?'

'Yes, your worship ; she could cook her wittles, but the poor young thing seemed never to have no heart for nothing, sir.'

'Never talked to you?'

'No, sir; nothing but cried. She cried, and cried, and cried, 'cept when she laughed, and then it were awful, your worship. My man always did say as how there was no knowing what she'd be doing of yet.'

'Is she married, do you know?'

'Yes, your worship; she wears her wedding-ring quite regular—only once she plucked it off and flung it in the fire—I saw it with my own eyes, sir, or I mightn't ha' believed it; and I never did see the like—but the poor creature's not re-sponsible at whiles—that's what my husband says.'

'What was her behaviour to the child? Did she seem fond of it?'

'Oh, yes, your worship; she used to hug, and hug, and hug it, and call it her darling, and Paul, and Paul, and Paul, and all she had left in the world.'

'When did you see her last before to-day?'

'Yesterday, sir; she put on her bonnet and cape and drew a shawl around the baby, and went out in the afternoon. "It will do you a mort of good," says I to her. "Yes, Mrs. Drayton," says she, "it will do us both a world of good." That was on the front doorsteps, your worship, and it were a nice afternoon, but I had never no idea what she meant to be doing of; but she's not responsible, poor young thing, that's what my——'

'And when night came and she hadn't got home, did you go in search of her?'

'Yes, your worship; for I says to my husband, says I, " Poor young thing, I can't rest in my bed, and knowing nothing of what's come to her." And my man he says to me, "Maggie," he says, " you go to the station and give the officers her description," he says—" a tall young woman

as might ha' been a born lady, a-carrying a
baby—that'll be good enough," he says, and
I went. And this morning the officer came,
and I knew by his face as something had
happened, and——'

'Let us hear the doctor. Is he in court?'

'Yes, your worship,' said the constable.

Mrs. Drayton was being bustled out of
the box. She stopped on the first step
down:

'And I do hope as no harm will come
to her—she's not responsible—that's what
my hus——'

'All right, we know all that; down with
you; this way; don't bother his worship!'

At the bottom of the steps the woman
stopped again, with a handkerchief to her
eyes.

'And it do make me cry to see her, poor
thing, and the baby, too, and innocent as a
kitten—and I hopes if anything is done to
her as——'

Mrs. Drayton's further hopes and fears
were lost in the bustle of the court.   The
young woman in the dock still gazed about
her vacantly.   There was strength in her
firmly-moulded lip, sensibility in her large
dark eyes, power in her broad, smooth brow,
and a certain stateliness in the outlines of
her tall, slim figure.

The doctor who had examined her gave
his report in a few words: the woman
should be under control, though she was
dangerous to no one but herself.   Her
attempt at suicide was one of the common
results of disaster in affairs of love.
Perhaps she was a married woman, abandoned by her husband; more likely she
was an unfortunate lady in whom the shame
of pregnancy had produced insanity.   She
was obviously a person of education and
delicacy of feeling.

'She must have connections of some
kind,' said the magistrate; and, turning to

the dock, he said quietly, 'Give us your name, my good lady.'

The woman seemed not to hear, but she clutched her child yet closer to her breast, and it cried feebly.

The magistrate tried again :

'Your baby's name is Paul, isn't it ? Paul—what ?'

She looked around, glanced at the magistrate and back at the people in the court, but said nothing.

Just then the door opposite the bench creaked slightly, and a gentleman entered. The woman's wandering eyes passed over him. In an instant her torpor was shaken off. She riveted her gaze on the new-comer. Her features contracted with lines of pain. She drew the child aside, as if to hide it from sight. Then her face twitched, and she staggered back into the arms of the constable behind her. She was now insensible. Through the dense folds of the fog the vague faces of the spectators showed an intent expression.

It was observed that the gentleman who had entered the court a moment before immediately left it. The magistrate saw him pass out of the door merely as a distorted figure in the dusky shadows.

'Let her be removed to the Dartford asylum,' said the magistrate; 'I shall give an order at once.'

A voice came from the body of the court. It was Mrs. Drayton's voice, thick with sobs.

'And if you please, your worship, may me and my husband take care of the child until the poor young thing is well enough to come for it? We've no children of our own, sir, and my husband and me, we'd like to have it, and no one would do no better by it, your worship.'

'I think you are a good woman, Mrs. Drayton,' said the magistrate. Then, turning to the clerk, he added, 'Let inquiries be made about her, and, if all prove satisfactory, let the child be given into her care.'

'Oh, thank your worship; it do make me cry——'

'Yes, all right—never mind now—we know all about it—come along.'

The prisoner recovered consciousness in being removed from the dock: the constable was taking the child out of her arms. She clung to it with feverish hands.

'He says I am not his wife,' she said in a deep whisper, and her eyes wandered to the door.

'Stop that man,' said the magistrate, pointing to the vague recesses into which the spectator had disappeared. An officer of the court went out hastily. Presently returning : 'He is gone,' said the officer.

'Take me away, take me away!' cried the prisoner in a tense voice. 'Paul, Paul, my own dear little Paul!' The woman's breath came and went in gusts, and her

child cried from the convulsive pressure to
her breast.

' Remove them,' said the bench.

There was a faint commotion. Among
the people in the court, huddled like sheep,
there was a harsh scraping of feet, and some
suppressed whispering. The stolid faces
on the bench turned and smiled slightly in
the yellow gleam of the gas that burned in
front of them. Then the momentary bustle
ended, the woman and child were gone, and
the calm monotony of the court was resumed.

Six months later a handsome woman,
still little more than a girl, yet with the
eyes of suffering, stepped up to the door of
a house in Pimlico and knocked timidly.

' I wish to see Mrs. Drayton,' she said,
when the door was opened by an elderly
person.

' Bless you, they're gone, Mrs. Drayton
and her husband.'

'Gone!' said the young woman, 'gone! What do you mean?'

'Why, gone—removed—shifted.'

'Removed—shifted?' The idea seemed to struggle its slow way into her brain.

'In course—what else, when the big hotel fails and he loses his job? Rents can't be paid on nothing a week, and something to put in the mouth besides.'

'Gone? Are you mad? Woman, think what you're saying. Gone where?'

'How do I know where? Mad, indeed! I'll not say but other folks look a mort madder nor ever I looked.'

The young woman took her by the shoulder. 'Don't say that—don't say you don't know where they're gone. They've got my child, I tell you; my poor little Paul.'

'Oh, so you're the young party as drownded herself, are you? Well, they're gone anyways, and the little chit with them, and there's no saying where. You may believe me. Ask the neighbours else.'

The young woman leaned against the door-jamb with a white face and great eyes.

'Well, well, how hard she takes it! Deary me, deary me, she's not a bad sort, after all. Well, well, who'd ha' thought it! There, there, come in and sit awhile. It *is* cruel to lose one's babby—and me to tell her, too. Misbegotten or not, it's one's own flesh and blood, and that's what I always says.'

The young woman had been drawn into the house and seated on a chair. She got up again with the face of an old woman.

'Oh, I'm choking!' she said.

'Rest awhile, do now, my dear—there—there.'

'No, no, my good woman, let me go.'

'Heaven help you, child; how you look!'

'Heaven has never helped me,' said the

young woman. 'I was a sister of charity only two years ago. A man found me and wooed me; married me and abandoned me; I tried to die and they rescued me; they separated me from my child and put me in an asylum; I escaped, and have now come for my darling, and he is gone.'

'Deary me, deary me!' and the old woman stroked her consolingly.

'Let me go,' she cried, starting up afresh. 'If Heaven has done nothing for me, perhaps the world itself will have mercy.'

The ghastly face answered ill to the grating laugh that followed as she jerked her head aside and hurried away.

CHAPTER I.

It was Young Folks' Day in the Vale of
Newlands. The summer was at its height;
the sun shone brightly; the lake to the
north lay flat as a floor of glass, and reflected
a continent of blue cloud; the fells were
clear to their summits, and purple with
waves of heather. It was noontide, and
the shadows were short. In the slumberous
atmosphere the bees droned, and the hot air
quivered some feet above the long, lush
grass. The fragrance of new-mown hay
floated languidly through a sub-current of
wild rose and honeysuckle. In a meadow
at the foot of the Causey Pike tents were

pitched, flags were flying, and crowds of men, women, and children watched the mountain sports.

In the centre of a group of spectators two men, stripped to the waist, were wrestling. They were huge fellows, with muscles that stood out on their arms like giant bulbs, and feet that held the ground like the hoofs of oxen. The wrestlers were calm to all outward appearance, and embraced each other with the quiet fondling of lambs and the sinuous power of less affectionate creatures. But the people about them were wildly excited. They stooped to watch every wary move‧ment of the foot, and craned their necks to catch the subtlest twist of the wrist.

' Sista, Reuben, sista ! He'll have enough to do to tummel John Proudfoot. John's up to the scat to-day, anyways.'

' Look tha ! John's on for giving him the cross-buttock.'

John was the blacksmith, a big, buirdly fellow with a large blunt head.

'And he has given it too, has John.'

'Nay, nay, John's doon—ey, ey, he's doon, is John.'

One of the wrestlers had thrown the other, and was standing quietly over him. He was a stalwart young man of eight-and-twenty, brown-haired, clear-eyed, of a ruddy complexion, with a short, thick, curly beard, and the grace of bearing that comes of health and strength, and a complete absence of self-consciousness. He smiled cheerfully, and nodded his head in response to loud shouts of applause. 'Weel done! Varra weel done! That's the way to ding 'em ower! What sayst tha, Reuben?'

'What a bash it was, to be sure!'

'What dusta think of yon wrustling, ey, man?'

'Nay, nay, it's varra middling.'

'Ever seen owt like it since the good

auld days you crack on sa often, auld
man ?'

' Nay, he doont him varra neat, did Paul
—I will allow it.'

' There's never a man in Cumberland
need take a hand with young Paul Ritson
after this.'

' Ey, ey ; he's his father's son.'

The wrestler, surrounded by a little multi-
tude of boys, who clung to his sparse
garments on every side, made his way to a
tent.

At the same moment a ludicrous figure
forced a passage through the crowd, and
came to a stand in the middle of the green.
It was a diminutive creature, mounted on a
pony that carried its owner on a saddle
immediately below its neck, and a pair of
panniers just above its tail. The rider was
an elderly man with shaggy eyebrows and
beard of mingled black and grey. His
swarthy, keen, wizened face was twisted

into grotesque lines beneath a pair of little
blinking eyes, which seemed constantly to
say that anybody who refused to see that
they belonged to a perfectly wideawake son
of old Adam made a portentous mistake.
He was the mountain pedlar, and to-day,
at least, his visit was opportune.

'Lasses, here's for you! Look you,
here's Gubblum Oglethorpe, pony and
all.'

'Why, didsta ever see the like—
Gubblum's getten hissel into a saddle!'

Gubblum, from his seat on the pony,
twisted one half of his wrinkled face awry
and said:

'In course I have! But it's a vast
easier getting into this saddle nor getting
out of it, *I* can tell you!'

'Why, how's that, Gubblum?' cried a
voice from the crowd.

'What, man, did you never hear of the
day I bought it?'

Sundry shakes of many heads were the response.

' No ?' said Gubblum, with an accent of sheer incredulity, and added, ' Well, there *is* no accounting for the ignorance of some folk.'

' What happened to you, Gubblum ?'

Gubblum's expression of surprise gave place to a look of condescension. He lifted his bronzed and hairy hand to the rim of his straw hat to shade his eyes from the sun.

' Well, when I got on to auld Bessy, here, I couldn't get off again—that's what happened.'

' No ? Why ?'

' You see, I'd got my clogs on when I went to buy the saddle in Kezzick, and they're middling wide in the soles, my clogs are. So when I put my feet into the stirrups, there they stuck.'

' Stuck !'

' Ey, fast as nails ! And when I got

home to Branth'et Edge I couldn't get them
out.   So our Sally, she said to my auld
woman, " Mother," she said, " we'll have
to put father into the stable with the pony
and fetch him a cup of tea."   And that's
what they did, and when I'd had summat
into me I had another fratch at getting out
of the saddle ; but I couldn't manish it ; so
I had—what do you think I had to do ?'

' Nay, man, what?'

' I had to sleep all night in the stable on
Bessy's back !'

' Bless   thee, Gubblum, and   whatever
didsta do ?'

' I'm coming to that, on'y some folks are
so impatient.   Next morning that lass of
mine she said to her mother, " Mother," she
said, " wouldn't it be best to take the saddle
off the pony, and then father he'll   sure
come off with it ?" '

'And did they do it ?'

' Ey, they did.   They took Bessy and

me round to the soft bed as they keeps maistly at the back of the stable, and they loosened the straps and gave a push, and cried " Away." '

' Weel, man, weel ?'

' *Weel!* nowt of the sort ! It wasn't *weel* at all ! When I rolled over I was off the pony, for sure ; but I was stuck fast to the saddle just the same.'

' Whatever did they do with thee then ?'

' I'm coming to that, too, on'y some folks are so mortal fond of hearing their- selves talk. They picked me up, saddle and all, and set me on the edge of the kitchen dresser. And there I sat for the best part of a week, sleeping and waking, and carding and spinning and getting fearful thin. But I got off at last, I did !'

There was a look of proud content in Gubblum's face as he added, ' What a thing it is to be eddicated ! We don't vally eddication half enough !'

A young fellow—it was Lang Geordie Moore—pushed a smirking face between the shoulders of two girls, and said, ' Did you take to reading and writing, then, Gubblum, when you were on the kitchen dresser ?'

There was a gurgling titter, but, disdaining to notice the interruption, Gubblum lifted his tawny face into the glare of the sun and said, ' It was my son as did it —him that is learning for a parson. He came home from St. Bees, and " Mother," he said, before he'd been in the house a minute, " let's take father's clogs off, and then his feet will come out of the stirrups." '

A loud laugh bubbled over the company. Gubblum sat erect in the saddle and added with a grave face : ' That's what comes of eddication and reading the Bible and all o' that ! If I had fifty sons I'd make 'em all parsons.'

The people laughed again, and crowed and exchanged nods and knowing winks. They enjoyed the pedlar's talk, and felt an indulgent tenderness for his slow and feeble intellect. He on his part enjoyed no less the assuming a simple and shallow nature. A twinkle lurked under his bushy brows while he 'smoked the gonies.' They laughed and he smiled slyly, and both were satisfied.

Gubblum Oglethorpe, pedlar, of Branth'et Edge, got off his pony and stroked its tousled mane. He was leading it to a temporary stable, when he met face to face the young wrestler, Paul Ritson, who was coming from the tent in his walking costume. Drawing up sharply, he surveyed Paul rapidly from head to foot, and then asked him with a look of bewilderment what he could be doing there.

'Why, when did you come back to these parts?'

Paul smiled. 'Come back! I've not been away.'

The old man looked slyly up into Paul's face and winked. Perceiving no response to that insinuating communication, his wrinkled face became more grave, and he said, 'You were nigh to London three days ago.'

'Nigh to London three days ago!' Paul laughed, then nodded across at a burly dalesman standing near, and said, 'Geordie, just pinch the old man, and see if he's dreaming.'

There was a general titter, followed by glances of amused inquiry. The pedlar took off his hat, held his head aside, scratched it leisurely, glanced up again into the face of young Ritson, as if to satisfy himself finally as to his identity, and eventually muttered half aloud, 'Well, I'm fair maizelt—that's what I am!'

'Maizelt—why?'

' I could ha' sworn I saw you at a spot near London three days ago.'

' Not been there these three years,' said Paul.

' Didn't you wave your hand to me as we went by—me and Bessy ?'

' Did I ?   Where ?'

' Why, at the " Hawk and Heron," in Hendon.'

' Never saw the place in my life.'

' Sure of that ?'

' Sure.'

The grave old head dropped once more, and the pony's head was held down to the withered hand that scratched and caressed it.   Then the first idea of a possible reason on Paul's part for keeping his movements secret suggested itself afresh to Gubblum. He glanced soberly around, caught the eye of the young dalesman furtively, and winked again.   Paul laughed outright, nodded his head good-humouredly, and rather ostenta-

tiously winked in response. The company
that had gathered about them caught the
humour of the situation, and tittered audibly enough to provoke the pedlar's
wrath.

'But I say you *have* seen it,' shouted
Gubblum in emphatic tones.

At that moment a slim young man walked
slowly past the group. He was well
dressed, and carried himself with ease and
some dignity, albeit with an air of listless-
ness—a weary and dragging gait, due in part
to a slight infirmity of one foot. When
some of the dalesmen bowed to him his
smile lacked warmth. He was Hugh Ritson, the younger brother of Paul.

Gubblum's manner gathered emphasis.
'You were standing on the step of the
"Hawk and Heron," said he, 'and I
waved my hand and shouted "A canny
morning to you, Master Paul!"—Ey, that
I did!'

'You don't say so!' said Paul with mock solemnity. His brother had caught the pedlar's words, and stopped.

'But I do say so,' said Gubblum, with many shakes of his big head. Let any facetious young gentleman who supposed that it was possible to make sport out of him, understand once for all that it might be as well to throw a stone into his own garden.

'Why, Gubblum,' said Paul, smothering a laugh, 'what was I doing at Hendon?'

'Doing! Well, a chap 'at was on the road along of me said that Master Paul had started innkeeper.'

There was a prolonged burst of laughter, amid which one amused patriarch on a stick shouted, 'Feel if tha's abed, Gubblum, ma man!'

'And if I *is* abed, it's better nor being in bed-lam, isn't it?' shouted the pedlar.

Paul came to the rescue of Gubblum's

humour. 'Never mind, my lad. It was somebody *like* me, no doubt.'

'Like you! It caps all. If it wasn't you, it must ha' been the old gentleman hissel'.'

'Are we so much alike? Come, let's see your pack.'

'His name was Paul, anyways.'

Hugh Ritson had elbowed his way through the group, and was now at Gubblum's elbow listening intently. When the others had laughed, he alone preserved an equal countenance.

'Paul—what?' he asked.

'Nay, don't ax me—I know nowt no mair—I must be an auld maizelin, I must for sure!'

Hugh Ritson turned on his heel and walked off.

CHAPTER II.

THE Vale of Newlands runs north and south. On its east bank rise the Cat Bell fells and the Eel Crags ; on the west rise Hindscarth and Robinson, backed by Whiteless Pike and Grasmoor. A river flows down the bed of the valley, springing in the south among the heights of Dale Head, and emptying into Bassenthwaite on the north. A village known as Little Town stands about midway in the vale, and a road runs along each bank. The tents were pitched for the sports near the bed of the valley, on the east side of the Newlands Beck. On the west side, above the road, there was a thick copse of hazel, oak, and birch.

From a clearing in this wood a thin column of pale blue smoke was rising through the still air. A hut in the shape of a cone stood a few yards from the road. It was thatched from the ground upwards with heather and bracken, leaving only a low aperture as door. Near the hut a small fire of hazel sticks crackled under a pot that swung from a forked triangle of oak limbs. Faggots were stacked at one end of the clearing; a pile of loose bark lay near. It was a charcoal pit, and behind a line of hurdles that were propped with poles and intertwined with dead grass and gorse, an old man was building a charcoal fire.

He was tall and slight, and he stooped. His eyes were large and heavy; his long beard was whitening. He wore a low-crowned hat with broad brim, and a loose flannel jacket without a waistcoat. Most of us convey the idea that to our own view

we are centres of our circles, and that the
universe revolves about us. This old man
suggested a different feel'ng. To himself
he might have been a thing gone somehow
out of its orbit. There was a listless
melancholy, a lonely weariness in his look
and movements. An old misery seemed to
sit on him.

His name was Matthew Fisher; but the
folk of the country-side called him Laird
Fisher. The dubious dignity came of the
circumstance that he was the holder of an
absolute royalty on a few acres of land
under Hindscarth. The royalty had been
many generations in his family. His grandfather had set store by it. When the Lord
of the Manor had worked the copper pits at
the foot of the Eel Crags, he had tried to
possess himself of the royalties of the
Fishers. But the peasant family resisted the
aristocrat. Luke Fisher believed there was
a fortune under his feet, and he meant to

try his own luck on his holding some day.
That day never came. His son, Mark
Fisher, carried on the tradition, but made
no effort to unearth the fortune. They
were a cool, silent, slow, and stubborn race.
Matthew Fisher followed his father and his
grandfather, and inherited the family faith.
All these years the tenders of the Lord of
the Manor were ignored, and the Fishers
enjoyed their title of courtesy or badinage.
When Matthew was a boy there was a
rhyme current in the vale which ran :

'There's t' auld laird, and t' young laird, and t' laird
   among t' barns,
If iver there comes another laird, we'll hang him up by
   t' arms.'

There is a tough bit of Toryism in the
grain of these northern dalesfolk. Their
threat was idle ; no other Laird ever came.
Matthew married, and had one daughter
only. He farmed his few acres with poor
results. The ground was good enough, but

Matthew was living under the shadow of the family tradition. One day—it was Sunday morning, and the sun shone brightly—he was rambling by the Po Beck that rose on Hindscarth and passed through his land, when his eye glanced over a glittering stone that lay among the pebbles at the bottom of the stream. It was ore, good full ore, and on the very surface. Then the Laird Fisher sank a shaft and all his earnings with it in an attempt to procure iron or copper. The dalespeople derided him, but he held silently on his way.

'How dusta find the cobbles to-day—any softer?' they would ask.

'As soft as the hearts of most folk,' he would answer, and then add in a murmur, 'and maybe a vast harder nor their heads.'

The undeceiving came at length, and then the Laird Fisher was old and poor. His wife died broken-hearted. After that the Laird never rallied. The breezy irony of the dalesfolk did not spare the old man's bent head. ' He's brankan' (holding up his head) ' like a steg swan,' they would say as he went past. The shaft was left unworked, and the holding lay fallow. Laird Fisher took wage from the lord of the manor to burn charcoal in the copse.

The old man had raised his vertical shaft, and was laying the oak limbs against it, when a girl of about eighteen came along the road from the south, and clambered over the stile that led to the charcoal pit. She was followed by a sheep-dog, small and wiry as a hill-fox.

' Is that thee, Mercy ?' said the charcoal-burner from the fire, without turning.

The girl was a pretty little thing; yet there was something wrong with her prettiness. One saw at once that her cheeks should have been pink and white like the daisy; and that her hair, which was yellow as the primrose, should have tumbled in

wavelets about them. There ought to have
been sunshine in the blue eyes, and laughter
on the red lips, and a merry lilt in the soft
voice. But the pink had faded from the
girl's cheek; the shadow had chased the
sunshine from her eyes; her lips had taken
a downward turn, and a note of sadness had
stolen the merriment from her voice.

'It's only your tea, father,' she said,
setting down a basket. Then, taking up a
spoon that lay on the ground, she stirred the
mess that was simmering over the fire.
The dog lay and blinked in the sun.

A rabbit rustled through the coppice, and
a jay screeched in the distant glade. But
above all came the peals of merry laughter
from below. The girl's eyes wandered
yearningly to the tents over which the flags
were flying.

'Do you hear the sports, father?' she
said.

'Ey, lass, there's gay carryin's on.

They're chirming and chirping like as many
sparrows.' The old man twisted about.
' I should have thowt as thou'd have been in
the thick of the thrang thysel, Mercy,
carryin' on the war.'

'I didn't care to go,' said Mercy in an
undertone.

The old man looked at her silently for a
moment.

' Ways me, but thoo's not the same heartsome lass,' he said, and went on piling the
faggots round the shaft. ' But *I* count
nowt of sec wark,' he added after a pause.

Little Mercy's eyes strayed back from the
bubbling pot to the tents below. There
was a shout of applause.

' That's Geordie Moore's voice,' thought
Mercy. She could see a circle with linked
hands. ' They're playing the cushion game,'
she said under her breath, and then drew a
long sigh.

Though she did not care to go to the sports

to-day, she felt, oh! so sick at heart. Like a wounded hare that creeps into quiet ambush, and lies down on the dry clover to die, she had stolen away from all this noisy happiness; but her heart's joy was draining away. In her wistful eyes there was something almost cruel in this bustling merriment, in this flaunting gaiety, in this sweet summer day itself.

The old charcoal-burner had stepped up to where the girl kneeled with far-away eyes.

' Mercy,' he said, ' I've wanted a word with you this many a day.'

' With me, father?'

The girl rose to her feet. There was a look of uneasiness in her face.

' You've lost your spirits—what's come of them?'

' Me, father?'

The assumed surprise was in danger of breaking down.

' Not well, Mercy—is that it ?'

He took her head between his hard old
hands, and stroked her hair as tenderly as a
mother.

' Oh yes, father, quite well, quite.'

Then there was a little forced laugh.
The lucent eyes were full of a dewy wistfulness.

' Any trouble, Mercy ?'

' What trouble, father ?'

' Nay, *any* trouble—trouble's common,
isn't it ?'

The old man's voice shook slightly, and
his hand trembled on the girl's head.

' What have *I* to trouble me ?' said Mercy
in a low voice nigh to breaking.

' Well, you know best,' said the charcoal-
burner. Then he put his hand under the
girl's chin and lifted her face until her un-
willing eyes looked into his. The scrutiny
appeared to console him, and a smile played
over his battered features. ' Maybe I was

wrong,' he thought. 'Folk are allus clattering.'

Mercy made another forced little laugh, and instantly the Laird Fisher's face saddened.

'They do say 'at you're not the same heartsome little lass,' he said.

'Do they? Oh, but I am quite happy! You always say people are busybodies, don't you, father?' The breakdown was imminent.

'Why, Mercy, you're crying.'

'Me—crying!' The girl tossed her head with a pathetic gesture of gay protestation. 'Oh no; I was laughing—that was it.'

'There are tears in your eyes, anyways.'

'Tears? Nonsense, father! Tears? Didn't I tell you that your sight was failing you—ey, didn't I, now?'

It was of no use to struggle longer.

The fair head fell on the heaving breast, and Mercy sobbed.

The old man looked at her through a blinding mist in his hazy eyes. 'Tell me, my little lassie, tell me,' he said.

'Oh, it's nothing,' said Mercy. She had brushed away the tears and was smiling.

The Laird Fisher shook his head.

'It's nothing, father—only——'

'Only—what?'

'Only—oh, it's nothing!'

'Mercy, my lass,' said the Laird Fisher, and the tears stood now in his own dim old eyes, 'Mercy, remember if owt goes wrong with a girl, and her mother is under the grass, her father is the first she should come to and tell all.'

The old man had seated himself on a stout block cut from a trunk, and was opening the basket, when there was a light springy step on the road.

' So you fire to-night, Matthew ?'

An elderly gentleman leaned over the stile and smiled.

' Nay, Mr. Bonnithorne, there's ower much nastment in the weather yet.'

The gentleman took off his silk hat and mopped his forehead. His hair was thin and of a pale yellow, and was smoothed flat on his brow.

' You surprise me. I thought the weather perfect. See how blue the sky is.'

' That doesn't argy. It might be better with never a blenk of blue. It was rayder airy yesterday, and last night the moon got up as blake and yellow as May butter.'

The smile was perpetual on the gentleman's face. It showed his teeth constantly.

' You dalesmen are so weather wise. Odd, isn't it ?' The voice was soft and womanish. There was a little laugh at the end of each remark.

'We go by the moon in firing, sir,' the charcoal-burner answered. 'Last night it rose nor'west, and that doesn't mean betterment, though it's quiet enough now. There'll be clashy weather before nightfall.'

The girl had strayed away into the thicket, and startled a woodcock out of a heap of dead oak leaves. The gentleman followed her with his eyes. They were very small and piercing eyes, and they blinked frequently.

'Your daughter does not look very well, Matthew?'

'She's gaily, sir, she's gaily,' said the charcoal-burner shortly, his mouth in his can of tea.

The gentleman smiled from the teeth out. After a pause he said, 'I suppose it isn't pleasant when one of your hurdles is blown down, and the charcoal burning,' indicating the arc of wooden hurdles which had been propped about the half-built charcoal stack.

'Ey, it's gay bad wark to be sure—being dragged into the fire.'

The dog had risen with a startled movement. Following the upward direction of the animal's nose, the gentleman said, 'Whose sheep are those in the ghyll yonder?'

'Auld Mr. Ritson's, them herdwicks.'

The sheep were on a ridge of shelving rock.

'Dangerous spot, eh?'

'Ey, it's a bent place. They're varra clammersome, the black faced sorts.'

'I'll bid you good-day, Matthew.' The yellow-haired elderly gentleman with the perpetual smile was moving off. He walked with a jerk and a spring on his toes. 'And mind you take your daughter to the new doctor at Keswick,' he said at parting.

'It's not doctoring that'll mend Mercy,' the charcoal-burner muttered, when the other had gone.

CHAPTER III.

JOSIAH BONNITHORNE was quite without kins-
people or connections. His mother had
been one of two sisters who lived by keeping
a small confectioner's shop in Whitehaven
and were devoted Methodists. The sisters
had formed views as to matrimony, and they
enjoyed a curious similarity of choice.
They were to be the wives of preachers.
But the opportunity was long in coming,
and they grew elderly. At length the
younger sister died, and so solved the
problem of her future. The elder sister
was left for two years more alone with her
confectionery. Then she married a stranger
who had come to one of the pits as gangs-

man. It was a sad falling off. But at all events the gangsman was a local preacher, and so the poor soul who took him for husband had effected a compromise with her cherished ideal. It turned out that he was a scoundrel as well, and had a wife living elsewhere. This disclosure abridged his usefulness among the brethren, and he fled. Naturally he left his second wife behind, having previously secured a bill of sale on her household effects. A few months elapsed, the woman was turned adrift by her husband's creditors, and then a child was born. It was a poor little thing—a boy. The good souls of the ' connection ' provided for it until it was two years old, and afterwards placed it in a charity school. While the little fellow was there, his mother was struck down by a mortal complaint. Then for the first time the poor ruined woman asked to see her child. They brought the little one to her bedside, and it smiled down into her dying face. ' Oh, that it may please the Lord to make him a preacher !' she said with a great effort. At a sign from the doctor the child was taken away. The face pinched by cruel suffering quivered slightly, the timid eyes worn by wasted hope softened and closed, and the mother bade farewell to everything.

The boy lived. They christened him Josiah, and he took for surname the maiden name of his mother, Bonnithorne. He was a weakling, and had no love of boyish sports; but he excelled in scholarship. In spite of these tendencies he was apprenticed to a butcher when the time came to remove him from school. An accident transferred him to the office of a solicitor, and he was articled. Ten years later he succeeded to his master's practice, and then he sailed with all sail set.

He disappointed the ' connection ' by

developing into a Churchman, but other-
wise aroused no hostile feeling. It was
obviously his cue to conciliate everybody.
He was liked without being popular, trusted
without being a favourite. Churchwarden,
trustee for public funds, executor for private
friends, he had a reputation for disinterested
industry. And people said how well it was
that one so unselfish as Josiah Bonnithorne
should nevertheless prosper even as this
world goes.

But there was a man in Cumberland who
knew Mr. Bonnithorne from the crown of
his head to the sole of his foot. That man
was Mr. Hugh Ritson. Never for an
instant did either of these palter with
the other.

When Mr. Bonnithorne left the charcoal-
pit, he followed the road that crossed the
Newlands Beck, and returned on the breast
of the Eel Crags. This led him close to the
booth where the sports were proceeding.

He heard as he passed the gurgling laugh with which the dalesfolk received the pedlar's story of how he saw Paul Ritson at Hendon. A minute afterwards he encountered Hugh Ritson on the road. There was only the most meagre pretence at greeting when these men came face to face.

'Your father sent for me,' said Mr. Bonnithorne.

'On what business?' Hugh Ritson asked.

'I have yet to learn.'

They walked some steps without speaking. Then the lawyer turned with his conventional smile, and said in his soft voice: 'I have just seen your little friend. She looks pale, poor thing. Something must be done, and shortly.'

Hugh Ritson's face flushed perceptibly. His eyes were on the ground.

'Let us go no farther in this matter,' he said in a low, deep tone. 'I saw her yesterday. Then there is her father, poor broken creature! Let it drop.'

'I did not believe it of you! Odd, isn't it?' Mr. Bonnithorne spoke calmly, and went on smiling.

'Besides, I am ashamed. The thing is too mean,' said Hugh Ritson. 'In what turgid melodrama does not just such an episode occur?'

'So, so! Such compunctious qualms! Or is it the story of the cat in the adage? You would and you wouldn't?'

'My blood is not thick enough, Bonnithorne. I can't do it.'

'Then why did you propose it? Was it your suggestion or mine? I thought to spare the girl her shame. Here her troubles must fall on her in battalions, poor little being. Send her away, and you decimate them.'

'It is unnecessary. You know I am superior to prejudice.' Hugh Ritson dropped his voice and said, as if speaking into his breast: 'If the worst comes to the worst I can marry her.'

Mr. Bonnithorne laughed lightly.

'Ho! ho! And in what turgid melodrama does not just such an episode occur?'

Hugh Ritson drew up sharply.

'Why not? Is she poor? Then what am I? Uneducated? What is education likely to do for me? A simple creature, all heart and no head? God be praised for that!'

At this moment a girl's laugh came rippling through the air. It was one of those joyous peals that make the heart's own music. Hugh Ritson's pale face flushed a little, and he drew his breath hard.

Mr. Bonnithorne nodded his head in the direction of the voice, and said softly: 'So our friend Greta is here to-day.'

'Yes,' said Hugh Ritson very quietly.

Mr. Bonnithorne's smile broadened. Then the friends walked some distance in silence.

'It is scarcely worthy of you to talk in this brain-sick fashion,' said Mr. Bonnithorne. There was a dull irritation in the tone. 'You place yourself in the wrong point of view. You do not love the little being.'

Hugh Ritson's forehead contracted, and he said : 'If I have wrecked my life by one folly, one act of astounding unwisdom, what matter ? There was but little to wreck. I am a disappointed man.'

'Pardon me, you are a very young one,' said the lawyer.

'What am I in my father's house ? He gives no hint of helping me to an independence in life.'

'There are the lands. Your father must be a rich man.'

'And I am a second son.'

' Indeed ?'

Hugh Ritson glanced up quickly.

' What do you mean ?'

' You say you are a second son.'

' And what then ?'

' You start. Would it be so fearful a thing if you were not a second son ?'

' In the name of truth, be plain. My brother Paul is living.'

Mr. Bonnithorne nodded his head twice or thrice, and said calmly : ' You know that your brother hopes to marry Greta ?'

' I have heard it.'

Again the flush came to Hugh Ritson's cheeks. His low voice had a tremor.

Mr. Bonnithorne laughed a little behind his teeth.

' Did I ever tell you of her father's strange legacy ?'

' Never.'

'My poor dead friend Robert Lowther left a handsome legacy to a son of his own, who was Greta's half-brother.'

'An illegitimate son?'

'Not strictly. Lowther married the son's mother,' said Mr. Bonnithorne.

'Married her? Then his son was his heir?'

'No.'

'No?'

Hugh Ritson looked perplexed.

'The girl was a Catholic, Lowther a Protestant. A Catholic priest married them in Ireland. That was not a valid marriage by English law.'

Hugh smiled grimly.

'And Lowther had the marriage annulled?'

'He had fallen in love,' began Mr. Bonnithorne.

'This time with an heiress?' There was a caustic laugh.

Mr. Bonnithorne nodded.   'Greta's mother.   So he——'

'Abandoned the first wife,' Hugh Ritson interrupted again.

Mr. Bonnithorne shook his head with an innocent expression.

'Wife?   Well, he left her.'

'You talk of a son.   Had they a child?'

'They. had,' said Mr. Bonnithorne, 'and when the woman and child . . . disappeared——'

'Exactly,' said Hugh Ritson, and he smiled.

The lawyer raised his head with a weak show of injured dignity.

'You wrong my dead friend by implication—the woman and child hid themselves.'

'What did Lowther then?'

'Married again, and had a daughter—Greta.'

'Then why the legacy?'

' Conscience-money,' said Mr. Bonnithorne, pursing up his mouth.

Hugh Ritson laughed slightly.

' The sort of fools' pence the Chancellor
of the Exchequer receives labelled " Income
Tax." '

' Precisely—only Lowther had no address
to send it to.'

' He had behaved like a scoundrel,' said
Hugh Ritson.

' True, and he felt remorse. After the
second marriage he set people to find the
poor woman and child. They were never
found. His last days were overshadowed
by his early fault. I believe he died
brokenhearted. In his will—I drew it for
him, poor dear Robert!—he left, as I say, a
handsome sum to be paid to this son of his
first wife—when found.'

Hugh Ritson laughed half mockingly.

' I thought he was a fool. A scoundrel
is generally a fool as well.'

' Generally; I've often observed it,' said Mr. Bonnithorne.

There was a momentary commerce of smiles.

' What possible interest of anybody's could it be to go hunting for the son of the fool's deserted wife ?'

' The fool,' answered Mr. Bonnithorne, ' was shrewd enough to make an interest by ordering that if the son were not found before Greta came of age, a legacy of double the sum should be paid to an orphanage for boys.'

Hugh Ritson's respect for the dead man's intelligence experienced a sensible elevation.

' So it is worth a legacy to the family to discover Greta's half-brother,' he said, summing up the situation in an instant.

' If alive—if not, then proof that he is dead.'

The two men had walked some distance,

and reached the turning of a lane which led to a house that could be seen among the trees at the foot of a gyhll. The younger man drew up on his infirm foot.

'But I fail to catch the relevance of all this. When I mentioned that I was a second son you——'

'I have had hardly any data to help me in my search,' Mr. Bonnithorne continued. He was walking on. 'Only a medallion-portrait of the first wife.' The lawyer dived into a breast-pocket.

'My brother Paul is living. What possible——'

'Here it is,' said Mr. Bonnithorne, and he held out a small picture.

Hugh Ritson took it with little interest.

'This is the portrait of a nun,' he said, as his eyes first fell on it, and recognised the coif and cape.

'A novice—that's what she was when Lowther met her,' said Mr. Bonnithorne.

Then Hugh Ritson stopped.   He regarded the portrait attentively; looked up
at the lawyer and back at the medallion.
For an instant the strong calm which he
had hitherto shown seemed to desert him.
The picture trembled in his hand.   Mr.
Bonnithorne did not appear to see his
agitation.

' Is it a fancy ?   Surely it must be a
fancy !' he muttered.

Then he asked aloud what the nun's
name had been.

' Ormerod.'

There was a start of recovered consciousness.

' Ormerod—that's strange !'

The exclamation seemed to escape in-
advertently.

' Why strange ?'

Hugh Ritson did not answer immediately.

' Her Christian name ?'

' Grace.'

' Grace Ormerod ? Why, you must know that Grace Ormerod happened to be my own mother's maiden name !'

' You don't say so ! Odd, isn't it ? You seem to recognise the portrait.'

Hugh Ritson had regained his self-possession. He assumed an air of in-difference.

' Well, yes—no, of course not—no,' he said emphatically at last.

In his heart there was another answer. He thought for the moment when he set eyes on the picture that it looked like—a little like—his own mother's face.

They walked on. Mr. Bonnithorne's perpetual smile parted his lips. Lifting his voice rather unnecessarily, he said :

' By the way, another odd coincidence ! Would you like to know the name of Grace Ormerod's child by Robert Lowther ?'

Hugh Ritson's heart leapt within him,

but he preserved an outward show of indifference, and drawled:

'Well, what was it?'

'Paul.'

The name went through him like an arrow. Then he said rather languidly:

'So the half-brother of Greta Lowther, wherever he is, is named——'

'Paul Lowther,' said Mr. Bonnithorne. 'But,' he added, with a quick glance, 'he may—I say he *may*—be passing by another name—Paul something else, for example.'

'Assuredly—certainly—yes—yes,' Hugh Ritson mumbled. His all-but impenetrable calm was gone.

They had reached the front of the house, and stood in a paved courtyard. It was the home of the Ritsons, known as the Ghyll, a long Cumbrian homestead of grey stone and green slate. A lazy curl of smoke was winding up from one chimney through the clear air. A gossamer net of the tangled boughs of a slim briar-rose hung over the face of a broad porch, and at that moment a butterfly flitted through it. The chattering of geese came from behind.

'Robert Lowther was the father of Grace Ormerod's child?' said Hugh Ritson vacantly.

'The father of her son Paul.'

'And Greta is his daughter? Is that how it goes?'

'That is so—and half-sister of Paul.'

Hugh Ritson raised his eyes to Mr. Bonnithorne's face. 'And of what age would Paul Lowther be now?'

'Well, older than you, certainly. Perhaps as old as—yes, perhaps as old—fully as old as your brother.'

Hugh Ritson's infirm foot trailed heavily on the stones. His lips quivered. For a moment he seemed to be rapt. Then he swung about and muttered:

'Tut, it isn't within belief. Trusted

home, it might betray a man, heaven only knows how deeply.'

Mr. Bonnithorne looked up inquiringly. 'Pardon me, I fail, as you say, to catch the relevance.'

'Mr. Bonnithorne,' said Hugh Ritson, holding out his hand, 'you and I have long been good friends, have we not?'

'Oh, the best of good friends.'

'At your leisure, when I have had time to think of this, let us discuss it further.'

Mr. Bonnithorne smiled assent. 'And meantime,' he said softly, 'let the unhappy little being we spoke of be sent away.'

Hugh Ritson's eyes fell, and his voice deepened. 'Poor little soul—I'm sorry—damnably.'

'As for Greta and her lover—well——' the lawyer nodded his head significantly, and left his words unfinished.

'My father is crossing the stackyard,'

said Hugh Ritson. 'You shall see him in good time. Come this way.'

The shadows were lengthening in the valley. A purple belt was stretching across the distant hills, and a dark blue tint was nestling under the eaves. A solitary crow flew across the sky, and cawed out its guttural note. Its shadow fell, as it passed, on two elderly people who were coming into the courtyard.

CHAPTER IV.

' It's time for that laal Mr. Bonnithorne to be here,' said Allan Ritson.

' Why did you send for him ?' asked Mrs. Ritson, in the low tone that was natural to her.

' To get that matter about the will off my mind. It'll be one thing less to think about, and it has boddert me sair and lang.'

Allan spoke with the shuffling reserve of a man to whose secret communings a painful idea had been too long familiar. In the effort to cast off the unwelcome and secret associate, there was a show of emancipation which, as an acute observer might see, was more reassumed than real.

Mrs. Ritson made no terms with the affectation of indifference. Her grave face became yet more grave, and her soft voice grew softer as she said, 'And if when it is settled and done the cloud would break that has hung over our lives, then all would be well! But that can never be!'

Allan tossed his head aside, and made pretence to smile; but no gleam of sunshine on his corn-fields was ever chased so closely by the line of dark shadow, as his smile by the frown that followed.

'Come, worrit thysel' na mair about it! When I've made my will, and put Paul on the same footing with t'other lad, who knows owt mair nor we choose to tell?'

Mrs. Ritson glanced into his face with a look of sad reproach. 'Heaven knows, Allan,' she said, 'and the dark cloud still gathers for us there.'

The old man took a step or two on the gravel path, and dropped his grey head. His voice deepened: 'Tha says reet, mother,' he said, ' tha says reet. Ey, it saddens my auld days—and thine forby!' He took a step or two more and added, ' And na lawyer can shak' it off now. Nay, nay, never now. Weel, mother, our sky has been lang owerkessen, but, mind ye,' lifting his face and voice together, ' we've had gude creps if we tholed some thistles.'

' Yes, we've had happy days too,' said Mrs. Ritson.

At that moment there came from across the vale the shouts of the merrymakers and the music of a fiddle. Allan Ritson lifted his head, nodded it aside jauntily, and smiled feebly through the mist that was gathering about his eyes.

' There they are—wrestling and jumping. I mind me when there was scarce a man in Cummerlan' could give me the cross-buttock.

That's many a lang year agone, though. And now our Paul can manish most on 'em—that he can.'

The fiddle was playing a country dance. The old man listened : his face broadened, he lifted a leg jauntily, and gave a sweep of one arm.

Just then there came through the air a peal of happy laughter. It was the same heart's music that Hugh Ritson and ·Mr. Bonnithorne had heard in the road. Allan's face brightened, and his voice had only the faintest crack in it as he said, ' That's Greta's laugh! It is for sure! What a heartsome lass yon is ! I like a heartsome lassie—a merry touch, and gone!'

' Yes,' said Mrs. Ritson soberly ; ' Greta is a winsome girl.'

It was hardly spoken when a young girl bounded down upon them, almost breathless, yet laughing in gusts, turning her head over her shoulder and shouting :

'Hurrah! Beaten, sir! Hurrah!'

It was Greta Lowther: twenty years of age, with fair hair, quick brown eyes, a sunny face lighted up with youthful animation, a swift smile on her parted lips—an English wild white rose.

'I've beaten him,' she said. 'He challenged me to cross Windybrowe while he ran round the Bowder stone, but I got to the lonnin before he had crossed the bridge.'

Then, running to the corner of the lane, she plucked off her straw hat, waved it about her head, and shouted again in an accent of triumph:

'Hurrah! hurrah! beaten, sir, beaten!'

Paul Ritson came running down the fell in strides of two yards apiece.

'Oh, you young rogue—you cheated!' he cried, coming to a stand and catching his breath.

'Cheated?' said Greta, in a tone of dire amazement.

'You bargained to touch the beacon on the top of Windybrowe, and you didn't go within a hundred yards of it.'

'The beacon? On Windybrowe?' said the girl, and wondrous perplexity shone in her lovely eyes.

Paul wiped his brow, and shook his head and his finger with mock gravity at the beautiful cheat.

'Now, Greta, now—now—gently——'

Greta looked round with the bewildered gaze of a lost lambkin.

'Mother,' said Paul, 'she stole a march on me.'

'He was the thief, Mrs. Ritson: you believe me, don't you?'

'Me? why I never stole anything in my life,—save one thing.'

'And what was that, pray?' said Greta, with another mighty innocent look.

Paul crept up to her side and whispered something over her shoulder, whereupon she eyed him largely, and said with a quick smile : ' You don't say so ! But *please* don't be too certain of it. I'm sure *I* never heard of that theft.'

' Then here's a theft you shall hear of,' said Paul, throwing one arm about her neck, and tipping up her chin.

There was a sudden gleam of rosy, roguish lips. Old Allan, with mischief dancing in his eyes, pretended to recover them from a more distant sight.

' Ey, why, what's that ?' he said, ' the sneck of a gate, eh ?'

Greta drew herself up. ' How can you,—and all the people looking—they might really think that we were—we were———'

Paul came behind, put his head over one shoulder, and said, 'And we're not, are we ?'

' They're weel matched, mother, eh ?' said Allan, turning to his wife. ' They're

marra-to-bran, as folk say. Greta, he's a
girt booby, isn't he?'

Greta stepped up to the old man, and
with a familiar gesture laid a hand on his
arm. At the same moment Paul came to
his side. Allan tapped his son on the back.
'Thou girt lang booby,' he said, and
laughed heartily. All the shadows that had
hung over him were gone. 'And how's
Parson Christian?' he asked in another
tone.

'Well, quite well, and as dear an old
soul as ever,' said Greta.

'He's father and mother to thee baith,
my lass. I never knew thy awn father.
He was dead and gone before we coom't to
these parts. And thy mother, too, God
bless her! she's dead and gone now. But
if this lad of mine, this Paul, this girt lang
—— Ah, and here's Mr. Bonnithorne, and
Hughie, too.'

The return of the lawyer and Hugh

Ritson abridged the threat of punishment that seemed to hang large on the old man's lips.

Hugh Ritson's lifted eyes had comprehended everything. The girl leaning over his father's arm; the pure smooth cheeks close to the swarthy, weather-beaten, comfortable old face; the soft gaze upwards full of feeling; the half open lips and the teeth like pearls; then the glance round, half of mockery, half of protest, altogether of unconquerable love, to where Paul Ritson stood, his eyes just breaking into a smile; the head, the neck, the arms, the bosom still heaving gently after the race; the light loose costume—Hugh Ritson saw it all, and his heart beat fast. His pale face whitened at that moment, and his infirm foot trailed heavily on the gravel.

Allan shook hands with Mr. Bonnithorne, and then turned to his sons. 'Come, you two lads, have no been gude friends latterly,

and that's a sair grief baith to your mother
and me.   You're not made in the same
mould seemingly.   But you must mak' up
your fratch, my lads, for your auld folk's
sake, if nowt else.'

At this he stretched out both arms, as if
with the intention of joining their hands.
Hugh made a gesture of protestation.

' I have no quarrel to make up,' he said,
and turned aside.

Paul held out his hand.   'Shake hands,
Hugh,' he said.   Hugh took the proffered
hand with unresponsive coldness.

Paul glanced into his brother's face a
moment, and said, ' What's the use of
breeding malice ? It's a sort of live stock
that's not worth its fodder, and it eats up
everything.'

There was a scarcely perceptible curl
on Hugh Ritson's lip, but he turned silently
away.   With head on his breast he walked
towards the porch.

' Stop.'

It was old Allan's voice.   The deep tone
betrayed the anger that was choking him.
His face was flushed, his eyes were stern,
his lips trembled.

' Come back and shak' hands wi' thy
brother reet.'

Hugh Ritson faced about, leaning heavily
on his infirm foot.   ' Why to-day more than
yesterday or to-morrow ?' he said calmly.

' Come back, I tell thee,' shouted the old
man more hotly.

Hugh maintained his hold of himself,
and said in a quiet and even voice, ' I am
no longer a child.'

' Then bear thysel' like a man—not like
a whipped hound.'

The young man shuddered secretly from
head to foot.   His eyes flashed for an
instant.   Then, recovering his self control,
he said, ' Even a dog would resent such
language, sir.'

Greta had dropped aside from the painful scene, and for a moment Hugh Ritson's eyes followed her.

'I'll have no sec worriment in my house,' shouted the old man in a broken voice. 'Those that live here must live at peace. Those that want war must go.'

Hugh Ritson could bear up no longer. 'And what is your house to me, sir? What has it done for me? The world is wide.'

Old Allan was confounded. Silent, dumb, with great staring eyes, he looked round into the faces of those about him. Then in thick choking tones he shouted, 'Shak' thy brother's hand, or thou'rt no brother of his.'

'Perhaps not,' said Hugh very quietly.

'Shak' hands, I tell thee.' The old man's fists were clenched. His body quivered in every limb.

His son's lips were firmly set; he made no answer.

Then the old man snatched from Mr. Bonnithorne the stick he carried. At this Hugh lifted his eyes sharply until they met the eyes of his father. Allan was transfixed. The stick fell from his hand. Then Hugh Ritson halted into the house.

'Come back, come back . . . my boy . . . Hughie . . . come back!' the old man sobbed out. But there was no reply.

'Allan, be patient, forgive him; he will ask your pardon,' said Mrs. Ritson.

Paul and Greta had stolen away. The old man was now speechless, and his eyes, bent on the ground, swam with tears.

'All will be well, please God,' said Mrs. Ritson. 'Remember, he is sorely tried, poor boy. He expected you to do something for him.'

'And I meant to, I meant to—that I did,' the father answered in a broken cry.

'But you've put it off, and off, Allan —like everything else.'

Allan lifted his hazy eyes from the ground, and looked into his wife's face. 'If it had been the other lad I could have borne it maybe,' he said feelingly.

Mr. Bonnithorne, standing aside, had been ploughing the gravel with one foot. He now raised his eyes and said, with his customary smile, 'And yet, Mr. Ritson, folk say that you have always shown most favour to your eldest son.'

The old man's gaze rested on the lawyer for a moment, but he did not speak. Mr. Bonnithorne went on smiling; and to break an awkward silence he added, 'Odd, isn't it?'

'I've summat to say to Mr. Bonnithorne, mother,' said the statesman. He was quieter now. Mrs. Ritson stepped into the house.

Allan Ritson and the lawyer followed her,

going into a little parlour to the right of the porch. It was a quaint room, full of the odour of a bygone time. The floor was of polished black oak, covered with skins ; the ceiling was of panelled oak, and had a panelled beam. Bright oak cupboards, their fronts carved with rude figures, were set into the walls, which were whitened, and bore one illuminated text and three prints in black and white. The furniture was heavy and old. There was a spinning-wheel under the wide window-board. A bluebottle buzzed about the ceiling ; a slant of sunlight crossed the floor. The men sat down.

'I sent for thee to mak' my will, Bonni-thorne,' said the old man.

The lawyer smiled.

'A necessary precaution, such as admits of no delay. It is a legal maxim that delay in affairs of law is a candle that burns in the daytime : when the night comes it is burnt to the socket.'

Old Allan took little heed of the sentiment.

'Ey,' he said, 'but there's mair nor common 'casion for it in my case.'

The lawyer was instantly on the alert.

'And what is your especial reason?' he asked.

Allan's mind seemed to wander. He stood silent for a moment, and then said slowly, as if labouring with thought and phrase :

'Weel, tha must know . . . I scarce know how to tell thee. . . . Weel, my eldest son, Paul as they call him——'

The old man stopped, and his manner grew sullen. Mr. Bonnithorne came to his help.

'Yes, I am all attention—your eldest son——'

'He is——he is——'

The door opened and Mrs. Ritson entered the room, followed close by the Laird Fisher.

'Mr. Ritson, your sheep, them black-

faced herdwicks on Hindscarth, have broken
the fences, and the red drift of 'em is down
in the barrowmouth of the pass,' said the
charcoal-burner.

The statesman got on his feet.

'I must gang away at once,' he said.
'Mr. Bonnithorne, I must put thee off, or
maybe I'll lose fifty head of sheep down in
the ghyll.'

'I made so bold as to tell ye, for I reckon
we'll have all maks of weathers yet.'

'Tha's reet, Mattha; and reet neigh-
bourly forby. I'll slip away after thee in a
thumb's snitting.'

The Laird Fisher went out.

'Can ye bide here for me until eight
o'clock to-neet, Mr. Bonnithorne?'

There was some vexation written on the
lawyer's face, but he answered with meek-
ness:

'I am always at your service, Mr. Ritson.
I can return at eight.'

'Varra good.' Then, turning to Mrs. Ritson, 'Give friend Bonnithorne a bite o' summat, said Allan, and he followed the charcoal-burner. Out in the courtyard he called the dogs. 'Hey howe! hey howe! Bright! Laddie! Come, boys, come, boys, te-lick, te-smack!'

He put his head in at the door of an outhouse and shouted, 'Reuben, whereiver ista? Come thy ways quick, and bring the lad!'

In another moment a young shepherd and a cowherd, surrounded by three or four sheep-dogs, joined Allan Ritson in the courtyard.

'Dusta gang back to the fell, Mattha?' said the statesman.

'Nay, I's done for the day. I'm away home.'

'Good-neet, and thank.'

Then the troop disappeared down the lonnin—the men calling, the dogs barking.

In walking through the hall Mr. Bonni-thorne encountered Hugh Ritson, who was passing out of the house, his face very hard, his head much bent.

'Would you,' said the lawyer, still meekly, 'like to know the business on which I have been called here?'

Hugh Ritson did not immediately raise his eyes.

'To make his will,' added Mr. Bonni-thorne, not waiting for an answer.

Then Hugh Ritson's eyes were lifted; there was one flash of intelligence; after that the young man went out without a word.

CHAPTER V.

HUGH RITSON was seven-and-twenty. His clean-shaven face was long, pale, and intellectual; his nose was wide at the bridge and full at the nostrils; he had firm-set lips, large vehement eyes, and a broad forehead, with hair of dark auburn parted down the middle and falling in thin waves on the temples. The expression of the physiognomy in repose was one of pain and in action of power; the effect of the whole was not unlike that which is produced by the face of a high-bred horse, with its deep eyes and dilated nostrils. He was barely above medium height, and his figure was almost delicate. When he spoke his voice

startled you—it was so low and deep to
come from that slight frame.　His lameness,
which was slight, was due to a long-stand-
ing infirmity of the hip.

As second son of a Cumbrian statesman,
whose estate consisted chiefly of land, he
expected but little from his father, and had
been trained in the profession of a mining
engineer.　After spending a few months at
the iron mines of Cleator, he had removed
to London at twenty-two, and enrolled himself as a student of the Mining College in
Jermyn Street.　There he had spent four
years, sharing the chambers of a young bar-
rister in the Temple Gardens.　His London
career was uneventful.　Taciturn in manner,
he made few friends.　His mind had a ten-
dency towards contemplative inactivity.　Of
physical energy he had very little, and this
may have been partly due to his infirmity.
Late at night he would walk alone in the
Strand: the teeming life of the city, and

the mystery of its silence after midnight, had a strong fascination for him. In these rambles he came to know some of the strangest and oddest of the rags and rinsings of humanity : among them a Persian noble-man of the late Shah's household, who kept a small tobacco-shop at the corner of a by-street, and an old French exile, once of the court of Louis Phillippe, who sold the halfpenny papers. At other times he went out hardly at all, and was rarely invited.

Only the housemate, who saw him at all times and in many moods, seemed to suspect that beneath that cold exterior there lay an ardent nature. But he himself knew how strong was the tide of his passion. He could never look a beautiful woman in the face but his pulse beat high, and he felt almost faint. Yet strong as his passion was, his will was no less strong. He put a check on himself, and during his four years in

London contrived successfully to dam up the flood that was secretly threatening him.

At six-and-twenty he returned to Cumberland, having some grounds for believing that his father intended to find him the means of mining for himself. A year had now passed, and nothing had been done. He was growing sick with hope deferred. His elder brother, Paul, had spent his life on the land, and it was always understood that in due course he would inherit it. That at least was the prospect which Hugh Ritson had in view, though no prospective arrangement had been made. Week followed week, and month followed month, and his heart grew bitter. He had almost decided to end this waiting. The day would come when he could bear it no longer, and then he would cut adrift.

An accidental circumstance was the cause of his irresolution. He used to walk

frequently on the moss where the Laird
Fisher sank his shaft. In the beck that
ran close to the disused head-gear he would
wade for an hour early in the summer
morning. One day he saw the old Laird's
daughter washing linen at the beck-side.
He remembered her as a pretty, prattling
thing of ten or eleven. She was now a
girl of eighteen, with a pure face, a timid
manner, and an air that was neither that of
a woman nor of a child. Her mother was
lately dead, her father spent most of his
days on the fell (some of his nights also
when the charcoal was burning), and she
was much alone. Hugh Ritson liked her
gentle replies and her few simple questions.
So it came about that he would look for her
in the mornings, and be disappointed if he
did not catch sight of her good young face.
Himself a silent man, he liked to listen to
the girl's modest, unconnected talk. His
stern eyes would soften at such times to a

sort of caressing expression. This went on for months, and in that solitude no idle tongue was set to wag. At length Hugh Ritson perceived that the girl's heart was touched. If he came late he found her leaning over a gate, her eyes bent down among the mountain grasses at her feet, and her cheeks coloured by a red glow. It is unnecessary to go farther. The girl gave herself up to him with her whole heart and soul, and he—well, he found the bulwarks with which he had surrounded himself were ruined and down.

Then the awakening came, and Hugh learned too late that he had not loved the simple child, by realizing that with all the ardour of his restrained but passionate nature he loved another woman.

So much for the first complication in the tragedy of this man's life.

The second complication was new to his consciousness, and it was at this moment conspiring with the first to lure him to consequences that are now to be related. The story which Mr. Bonnithorne had told of the legacy left by Greta's father to a son by one Grace Ormerod had come to him at a time when, owing to disappointment and chagrin, he was peculiarly liable to the temptation of any 'honest trifle' that pointed the way he wished to go. If the Grace Ormerod who married Lowther had indeed been his own mother, then—a thousand to one—Paul was Lowther's son. If Paul was Lowther's son, he was also half-brother of Greta. If Paul was not the son of Allan Ritson, then he himself, Hugh Ritson, was his father's heir.

In the present whirlwind of feeling he did not inquire too closely into the pros and cons of probability. Enough that evidence seemed to be with him, and that it transformed the world in his view.

Perhaps the first result of this transforma-

tion was that he unconsciously assumed a
different attitude towards the unhappy
passage in his life wherein Mercy Fisher
was chiefly concerned. What his feeling
was before Mr. Bonnithorne's revelation,
we have already seen. Now the sentiment
that made much of such an ' accident ' was
fit only for a ' turgid melodrama,' and the
idea of ' atonement ' by ' marriage ' was
the mock heroic of those ' great lovers of
noble histories,' the spectators who applaud
it from the pit.

When he passed Mr. Bonnithorne in the
hall at the Ghyll he was on his way to the
cottage of the Laird Fisher. He saw in
the road ahead of him the group which
included his father and the charcoal-burner,
and to avoid them he cut across the breast of
the Eel Crags. After a sharp walk of a
mile he came to a little whitewashed house
that stood near the head of Newlands,
almost under the bridge that crosses the

fall. It was a sweet place in a great solitude, where the silence was broken only by the tumbling waters, the cooing of pigeons on the roof, and the twittering cf ringouzels by the side of the torrent. The air was fresh with the smell of new peat. There was a wedge-shaped garden in front, and it was encompassed by chestnut trees. As Hugh Ritson drew near he noticed that a squirrel crept from the fork of one of these trees. The little creature rocked itself on the thin end of a swaying branch, plucking sometimes at the drooping fan of the chestnut, and sometimes at the prickly shell of its pendulous nut. When he opened the little gate Hugh Ritson observed that a cat sat sedately behind the trunk of that tree, glancing up at intervals at the sporting squirrel in her moving seat.

As he entered the garden Mercy was crossing it with a pail of water just raised from the well. She had seen him, and now tried to pass into the house. He stopped before her and she set down the pail. Her head was held very low, and her cheeks were deeply flushed.

'Mercy,' he said, ' it is all arranged. Mr. Bonnithorne will see you into the train this evening, and when you get to your journey's end the person I spoke of will meet you.'

The girl lifted her eyes beseechingly to his face.

'Not to day, Hugh,' she said in a broken whisper; ' let me stay until to-morrow.'

He regarded her for a moment with a steadfast look, and when he spoke again his voice fell on her ear like the clank of a chain.

'The journey has to be made. Every week's delay increases the danger.'

The girl's eyes fell again, and the tears began to drop from them on to the brown arms that she had clasped in front.

'Come,' he said in a softer tone, 'the train starts in an hour. Your father is not yet home from the pit, and most of the dalespeople are at the sports. So much the better. Put on your cloak and hat and take the fell path to the Coledale road-ends. There Mr. Bonnithorne will meet you.'

The girl's tears were flowing fast, though she bit her lip and struggled to check them.

'Come, now, come; you know this was of your own choice.'

There was a pause. 'I never thought it would be so hard to go,' she said at length.

He smiled feebly, and tried a more rallying tone. 'You are not going for life. When your little trouble is over you will come back safe and happy.'

The words thrilled her through and through. Her clasped hands trembled visibly, and her fingers clutched them with a convulsive movement. After a while she was calmer, and said quietly : ' No, I'll never come back—I know that quite well.' And her head dropped on her breast and she felt sick at heart. ' I'll have to say good-bye to everything. There were Bessy Jackson's children—I kissed them all this morning, and never said why—little Willy. he seemed to know, dear little fellow, and cried so bitterly.'

The memories of these incidents touched to overflowing the springs of love in the girl's simple soul, and the bubbling child-voice was drowned in sobs.

The man stood with a smile of pity on his face. He came close, and brushed away her tears, and touched her drooping head with a gesture of protestation.

Mercy regained her voice. ' And then there's your mother,' she said, ' and I can't say good-bye to her, and my poor father, and I daren't tell him——'

Hugh stamped on the path impatiently.
' Come, come, Mercy, don't be foolish.'

The girl lifted to his the good young face
that had once been bonny as the day and
was now pale with weeping and drawn
down with grief. She took him by the
coat, and then, by an impulse which she
seemed unable to resist, threw one arm
about his neck, and raised her face to his
until their lips all but touched, and their
eyes met in a steadfast gaze.

' Hugh,' she said passionately, ' are you
sure that you love me well enough to think
of me when I am gone?—are you quite,
quite sure ?'

' Yes, yes; be sure of that,' he said
gently.

He disengaged her arm.

' And will you come and fetch me after
—after——'

She could not say the word. He smiled
and finished it.

7—2

' After *somebody* has come ?   Why, yes.'

Her fingers trembled and clung together ;
her head fell ; her cheeks were aglow.

' Why, of course.'   He smiled again, as
if in deprecation of so much childlike
earnestness ; then put his arm about the
girl's shoulder, dropped his voice to a tone
of mingled compassion and affection, and
said, as he lifted the brightening face to his,
' There, there—now go off and make
ready.'

The girl brushed her tears away vigorously, and looked half ashamed and half
enchanted.

' I'm going.'

' That's a good little girl.'

How the sunshine came back at the sound
of his words !

' Good-bye for the present, Mercy—only
for the present, you know !'

But how the shadow pursued the sunshine after all !

Hugh saw the tears gathering again in the lucent eyes, and came back a step.

There—a smile—just one little smile!' She smiled through her tears. 'There—there—that's a dear little Mercy. Good-day; good-bye.'

Hugh turned on his heel, and walked sharply away. As he passed out through the gate he could not help observing that the cat from the foot of the chestnut tree was walking stealthily off, with something like a dawning smile on its whiskered face, and the brush of the squirrel between its teeth.

Hugh Ritson had gained his end, and yet he felt more crushed than at the darkest moment of defeat. He had conquered his own manhood; and now he crept away from the scene of his triumph with a sense of utter abasement. When he had talked with Mr. Bonnithorne it was with a feeling of the meanness of the folly in which he was involved; and if any sentiment touching the girl's situation was strong upon him, it was closely bound up with a personal view of the degradation that might come of a gentleman's humiliating unwisdom. The very conventionality of his folly had irked him. But its cowardice was now uppermost. That a man should enter into warfare with a woman on unequal terms, and win by cajolery and deceit, was more than cruel: it was brutal. He could have borne even this hard saying so far as it concerned the woman's suffering, but for the reflection that it made the man something worse than a coxcomb in his own eyes.

The day was now far spent; the brilliant sun had dipped behind Grisedale, and left a ridge of dark fells in the west. On the east the green sides of Cat Bells and the Eel Crags were yellow at the summit, where the hills held their last commerce with the hidden sun. Not a breath of wind; not the rustle of a leaf: the valley lay still, save for the echoing voices of the merry-makers in the booths below. The sky overhead was blue, but a fibrous dark cloud, like the hulk of a ship, had anchored lately to the north.

Hugh Ritson took the valley road back to the Ghyll. He was visibly perturbed, he walked with head much bent, stopped suddenly at times, then snatched impetuously at the trailing bushes, and passed on. When he was under Hindscarth the sharp yap of dogs, followed by the bleat of unseen sheep, caused him to look up, and he saw a group of men, like emmets creeping on a dark boulder, moving over a ridge of shelving rock.

There was a slight spasm of his features at that moment, and his foot trailed more heavily as he went on. At a twist of the road he passed the Laird Fisher. The old man looked less melancholy than usual. It was as if the familiar sorrow sat a little more lightly to-night on the half-ruined creature.

'Good-neet to you, sir, and how fend ye?' hs said almost cheerily.

Hugh Ritson responded briefly. 'So you're not sleeping on the fell to-night, Matthew?' and as he spoke his eyes wandered towards the fell road.

'Nay; I's not firing to-neet, for sure; my daughter is expecting me.'

Hugh's eyes were now fixed intently on the road that crossed the foot of the fell to the west. The charcoal-burner was moving off, and, following at the same moment the upward direction of Hugh Ritson's gaze, he said, 'It's a baddish place yon, where your father is with Reuben and the lad, and it's baddish weather that is coming, too—look at yon black cloud over Walna Scar.'

Then for an instant there was embarrassment in Hugh Ritson's eyes. He answered in a faltering commonplace :

' Ways me ; but I must slip away home, sir ; my laal lass will be weary waiting. Good-neet to you, sir ; good-neet.'

' Good-night, Matthew, and God help you,' said Hugh, in a tone of startling earnestness, his eyes turned away.

He had walked half a mile further, and reached the lonnin that led to the Ghyll, when he was almost over-run by Greta Lowther, who came tripping out of the gate of a meadow, her bonnet swinging over her arm, her soft, wavy hair floating over her white forehead, her cheeks coloured with a warm glow, a roguish light in her eyes, and laughter on the point of bubbling out of her lips.

Greta had just given Paul Ritson the slip. There was a thicket in the field she had crossed, and it was covered with wild roses, white and red. Through the heart of it there rippled a tiny streak of water that was amber-tinted from the round shingle in its bed. The trunk of an old beech lay across it for ford or bridge. Underfoot were the sedge and the moss; overhead the thick boughs and the roses; in the air, the odour and the songs of birds. And Paul, the cunning rascal, would have tempted Greta into this solitude; but she was too shrewd, the wise little woman, to be so easily trapped. Pretending to follow him in ignorance of his manifest design, she had tripped back on tiptoe, and fled away like a lapwing over the noiseless grass.

When Greta met Hugh Ritson she was saying to herself of Paul in particular, and of his sex in general: 'What dear, simple, unsuspecting, trustful creatures they are!' Then she drew up sharply, 'Ah, Hugh!'

'How happy you look, Greta!' he said, fixing his eyes upon her.

A new light brightened her sunny face. 'Not happier than I feel,' she answered. She swung the arm over which the bonnet hung; the heaving of her breast showed the mould of her early womanhood.

Hugh Ritson's mind had for the last half-hour brooded over many a good purpose, but not one of them was now left.

'You witnessed a painful scene to-day,' he said with some hesitation. 'Be sure it was no less painful to me because you were there to see it.'

'Oh, I was so sorry,' said Greta impetuously. 'You mean with your father?'

Hugh bent his head slightly. 'It was inevitable—I know that full well—but for my share in it I ask your pardon.'

'That is nothing,' she said; 'but you took your father too seriously.'

'I took him at his word—that was all.'

'But the dear old man meant nothing; and you meant very much. He only wanted to abuse you a little, and perhaps frighten you, and shake his stick at you, and then love you all the better for it.'

'You may be right, Greta. Among the whims of nature there is that of making such human contradictions; but, as you say, I take things seriously—everything—life itself.'

He paused, and there was a slight trembling of the lip.

'Besides,' he went on in another tone, 'it has been always so. Since our child-hood—my brother's and mine—there has not been much parental tenderness wasted on *me*. I can hardly expect it now.'

'Surely that must be a morbid fancy,' Greta said in a distressed tone. The light was dying out of her eyes. She made one quick glance downward to where Hugh Ritson's infirm foot trailed on the road, and

then, in an instant of recovered consciousness, she glanced up, now confused and
embarrassed, into his face.

She was too late : he had read her
thought. A faint smile parted his lips,
and the light of his own eyes was cold.

' No ; not that,' he said ; ' I ask no pity
in that regard—and need none. Nature
has given my brother a physique that
would shame a Greek statue, but he and I
are quits—perhaps *more* than quits.'

He made a hard smile, and she flushed
deep with the shame of having her thought
read.

' I am sorry if I conveyed that,' she
said slowly. ' It must have been quite
unwittingly. I was thinking of your
mother. She is so good and tender to
everybody. Why, she is the angel of the
country-side. Do you know what name
they've given her ?'

Hugh shook his head.

'Saint Grace! Parson Christian told me—it seems it was my own dear mother who christened her.'

'Nevertheless there has not been much to sweeten my life, Greta,' he said.

His voice arrested her; it was charged with unusual feeling. She made no answer, and they began to walk towards the house.

After a few steps Greta remembered the trick that she had played on Paul, and craned her beautiful neck to see over the stone cobble-hedge into the field where she had left him.

Hugh observed her intently.

'I hear that you have decided. Is it so, Greta?' he said.

'Decided what?' she asked, colouring again.

He also coloured slightly, and answered with a strained quietness:

'To marry my brother.'

'If he wishes it—I suppose he does—
he says so, you know.'

Hugh looked earnestly into the girl's
glowing face, and said with deliberation:

'Greta, perhaps there are reasons why
you should not marry Paul.'

'What reasons?'

He did not reply at once, and she repeated her question. Then he said in a
strange tone:

'Just and lawful impediments, as they
say.'

Greta's eyes opened wide in undisguised
amazement.

'Impossible—you cannot mean it,' she
said with her customary impetuosity. She
glanced into Hugh's face, and misread what
she saw there. Then she began to laugh,
at first lightly, afterwards rather boisterously, and said with head averted, and
almost as if talking to herself, 'No, no;
he is nothing to me but the man I love.'

'Do you then love him ?'

Greta started.

'Do you ask?' she said.   The amazement in the wide eyes had deepened to a
look of rapture.   'Love him?' she said;
'better than all the world beside.'   The
girl was lifted out of herself.   'You are to
be my brother, Hugh, and I need not fear
to speak so.'

She swung her bonnet on her arm, just
to preserve composure by some distracting
exercise.

Hugh Ritson stopped, and his face
softened.   It was a perplexing smile that
sat on his features.   While he had talked
with Greta there had run through his mind,
as a painful undertone, the thought of
Mercy Fisher.   He had now dismissed the
last of his qualms respecting her.   To be
tied down for life to a mindless piece of
physical prettiness—what man of brains
could bear it ?   He had yielded to a natural

impulse—true! That moment of temptation threatened painful consequences—still
true! What then? Nothing! Was the
dead fruit to hang about his neck for ever?
Tut—all natural law was against it. Had
he not said that he was above prejudice?
So was he above the maudlin sentiment of
the 'great lovers of noble histories.' The
sophistry grew apace with Greta's beautiful
countenance before him. Catching at her
last word he said:

'Your brother—yes. But did you never
guess that I could have wished another
name?'

The look of amazement returned to her
eyes; he saw it and went on:

'Is it possible that you have not yet
read my secret?'

'What secret?' she said in a half-
smothered voice.

'Greta, if your love had been great love,
you must have read my secret just as I

have read yours.' In a low tone he continued, 'Long ago I knew that you loved, or thought you loved, my brother. I saw it before he had seen it—before you had realized it.'

The red glow coloured her cheeks more deeply than before. She had stopped, and he was tramping nervously backwards and forwards.

'Greta,' he said again, and he fixed his eyes entreatingly upon her, 'what is the love that scarcely knows itself?—that is the love with which you love my brother. And what is the tame, timid passion of a man of no mind?—that is the love which he offers you. What is your love for him, or his for you?—what is it, *can* it be? Love is not love unless it is the love of true minds. That was said long ago, Greta, and how true it is!' He went on quickly, in a tone of dull irritation, 'All other love is no better than lust. Greta, *I* understand you. It is not for a rude man like my brother to do so.' Then in an eager voice he said, 'Dearest, I bring you a love undreamt of among these country boors.'

'Country boors!' she repeated in a half-stifled whisper.

He did not hear her. His vehement eyes swam, and he was dizzy.

'Greta, dearest, I said there had been little in my life to sweeten it. Yet I am a man made to love and to be loved. My love for you has been mute for months ; but it can be mute no longer. Perhaps I have had my own impediment, apart from your love for Paul. But that is all over now.' Then with an impatient gesture he went on, 'I am tired of this place. To drag out one's days amid sheep and goats, and men and women as brainless, is not to live—it is only to exist.'

His cheeks quivered, his lips trembled, his voice swelled, his nervous fingers were

riveted to his palm. He approached her
and took her hand. She seemed to be
benumbed by strong feeling.

'Greta, you shall come with me! We
shall leave this slough where the pulse
scarcely beats and the mind stagnates.'

She had stood as one transfixed, a slow
paralysis of surprise laying hold of her
faculties. But at his touch her senses
regained their mastery. She flung away
his hand. Her breast heaved. In a voice
charged with indignation she said :

'So this is what you mean! I understand you at last!'

Hugh Ritson fell back a pace.

'Greta, hear me—hear me again!'

But she had found her voice indeed.

'Sir, you have outraged your brother's
heart as surely as if at this moment I had
been your brother's wife.'

'Greta, think before you speak—think,
I implore you.'

'I *have* thought! I have thought of you as your sister might think, and spoken to you as my brother. Now I know how mean of soul you are.'

Hugh broke in passionately:

'For God's sake stop! I am an unforgiving man—heaven made me so.' His nostrils quivered, every nerve vibrated.

'Love? You have never loved. If you knew what the word means you would die of shame where you stand this instant.'

Hugh lost all control.

'I bid you beware,' he said, in wrath and dismay.

'And I bid you be silent,' said Greta, with an eloquent uplifting of the hand. 'You offer your love to a pledged woman. It is only base love that is basely offered. It is bad coin, sir, and goes back dishonoured.'

Hugh Ritson regained some self-command. The contractions were deep about his forehead, but he answered in an imperturbable voice :

'You shall never marry my brother.'

'I shall—God willing.'

'Then you shall marry him to your life-long horror and disgrace.'

'That shall be as heaven may order.'

'A boor—a hulking brute—a bas——'

'Enough! I would rather marry a ploughboy than such a *gentleman* as you.'

Face to face, eye to eye, with panting breath and scornful looks, there they stood for one moment. Then Greta swung about and walked down the lonnin.

Hugh Ritson's natural manner returned instantly. He looked after her without the change of a feature, and then turned quietly into the house.

CHAPTER VI.

THERE was a drowsy calm in the room where Mr. Bonnithorne sat at lunch. It was the little oak-bound parlour to the right, in which he had begun the conversation with old Allan Ritson that had been interrupted by the announcement of the Laird Fisher. Half of the window was thrown up, and the landscape framed by the sash lay still as a picture. The sun that had passed over Grisedale sent a deep glow from behind, and the woods beneath took a restful tone. Only the mountain-head was aglow where it towered into the sky and the silence.

Mrs. Ritson entered and sat down. Her

manner was meek almost to abjectness. She was elderly, but her face bore traces of the beauty she had enjoyed in youth. The lines had grown deep in it since then, and now the sadness of its expression was permanent. She wore an old-fashioned lavender gown, and there was a white silk scarf about her neck. Her voice was low and tremulous, yet eager, and as if it were always questioning.

With downcast head, and eyes bent on her lap, where her fingers twitched nervously as she knitted without cessation, she sat silent, or put meek questions to her guest.

Mr. Bonnithorne answered in smiles and speeches of six words apiece. Between each sparse reply he addressed himself afresh to his lunch with an appetite that was the reverse of sparse. All the while a subdued hum of many voices came up from the booth in the fields below.

At length Mrs. Ritson's anxiety overcame the restraint of her manner.

'Mr. Bonnithorne,' she said, 'do let the will be made to-night. Urge Mr. Ritson, when he returns, to admit of no further delay. He has many noble qualities, but procrastination is his fault. It has been ever so.'

Mr. Bonnithorne paused with a glass half-raised to his lips, and lifted his eyes instead.

'Pardon me, madam,' he said, with the customary smile which failed to disarm his words; 'this is not a woman's business.' And just then a peacock strutted through the courtyard, startling the still air with its empty scream.

Mrs. Ritson coloured deeply. Even modesty like hers had been put to a severe strain. But she dropped her eyes again, finished a row of stitches, rested the steel needle on her lip, and answered quietly:

'Surely a woman may talk of what concerns her husband and her children.'

The great **man** had resumed his knife and fork. 'Not necessarily,' he said. 'It is a strange fact, unknown to most of your sex, that there is one condition in which the law does not recognise the right of a woman to call her son her own.'

During this prolonged speech, Hugh Ritson, fresh from his interview with Greta Lowther, entered the room, and stretched himself on the couch.

Mrs. Ritson, without shifting the determination of her gaze from the nervous fingers in her lap, said, 'What condition?'

Mr. Bonnithorne twisted slightly, and glanced significantly at Hugh as he answered, 'The condition of illegitimacy.'

Something supercilious in the tone jarred on Mrs. Ritson's ear. She looked up from her knitting and said, 'What do you mean?'

Bonnithorne placed his knife and fork with precision over his empty plate, used his napkin with deliberation, coughed slightly, and said, 'I mean that the law denies the name of son to offspring that has been bastardised.' Then, with another smile and a fresh glance at Hugh, he added, 'Odd, isn't it?'

Mrs. Ritson's face grew crimson, and she rose to her feet.

'If so, the law is cruel and wicked,' she said in a voice more tremulous with emotion.

Mr. Bonnithorne leaned languidly back in his chair, ejected a long 'hem' from his overburdened chest, inserted his fingers in the armpits of his waistcoat, looked up and said, 'Madam, it is a time-honoured maxim in law as in theology, that your women, like your clowns in the play, shall say no more than is set down for them. Odd, isn't it?'

Unluckily for the full effect of Mr. Bonnithorne's witticism, Paul Ritson, with Greta
at his side, appeared in the doorway at the
moment of its delivery.   The manner more
than the words had awakened his anger,
and the significance of both he interpreted
by his mother's agitated face.   In two
strides he stepped up to where the great
man sat, even now all smiles and white
teeth, and laid a powerful hand on his
arm.

'My friend,' said Paul lustily, 'it might
not be safe for you to speak to my mother
again like that.'

Mr. Bonnithorne rose stiffly, and his
shifty eyes looked into Paul's wrathful
face.

'Safe ?' he echoed with emphasis.

Paul, his lips compressed, bent his head,
and at the same instant brought the other
hand down on the table.

Without speaking, Mr. Bonnithorne

shuffled back into his seat. Mrs. Ritson, letting fall her knitting into her lap, sat and dropped her face into her hands. Paul took her by the arm, raised her up, and led her out of the room. As he did so he passed the couch on which Hugh Ritson lay, and looked down with mingled anger and contempt into his brother's indifferent eyes.

When the door closed behind them, Hugh Ritson and Mr. Bonnithorne rose together. There was a momentary gleam of mutual consciousness. Then instantly, suddenly, by one impulse, the two men joined hands across the table.

THE cloud that had hung over Walna Scar broke above the valley, and a heavy rainstorm, with low mutterings of distant thunder, drove the pleasure-people from the meadow to the booth. It was a long canvas tent with a drinking bar at one end, and stalls in the corners for the sale of gingerbreads and gimcracks. The grass under it was trodden flat, and in patches the earth was bare and wet beneath the traipseing feet of the people. They were a mixed and curious company. In a ring that was cleared by an athletic ploughman the fiddler-postman of Newlands, Tom o' Dint, was seated on a tub turned bottom

up. He was a little man with bowed legs
and feet a foot long.

'Now, lasses, step forret. Dunnot be
blate.'

'Come along with ye, any as have
springyness in them.'

The rough invitation was accepted without too much timidity by several damsels
dressed in gorgeous gowns and bonnets.
Then up and down, one, two, three, cut and
shuffle, cross, under, and up and down again.

'I'll be mounting my best nag and
comin' ower to Scara Crag and tappin' at
your window some neet soon,' whispered a
young fellow to the girl he had just danced
with.

She laughed a little mockingly.

'*Your* best nag, Willy?'

'Weel — the maister's.' She laughed
again, and a sneer curled her lip. 'You
Colebank chaps are famous sweethearters, I
hear. Fare-te-weel, Willy.'

And she twisted on her heel. He followed her up.

'Dunnet gowl, Aggy. Mappen I'll be maister man mysel' soon.'

Aggy pushed her way through the crowd and disappeared.

'She's packed him off wi' a flea in his ear,' said an elderly man standing near.

'Just like all the lave of them,' said another, 'snurling up her neb at a man for lack of gear. Why didna he brag of some rich uncle in Austrilly?'

'Ey, and stuff her with all sorts of flaitchment and lies. Then all the lasses wad be glyming at him.'

The dance span on.

'Why, it's a regular upshot, as good as Carel fair,' said one of the girls.

'Bessie, you're reet clipt and heeled for sure,' responded her companion.

Bessie's eyes sparkled with delight at the lusty compliment paid to her dancing, and she opened her cloak to cool herself, and also to show the glittering locket that hung about her neck.

'It's famish, this fashion,' muttered the elderly cynic. 'It must tak' a brave canny fortune.'

'Shaf, man, the country's puzzen'd round with pride,' answered his gossip. 'Lasses worked in the old days. Now they never do a hand's turn but washin' and bleachin' and starchin' and curling their polls.'

'Ey, ey, there's been na luck in the country since the women folk began to think shame of their wark.'

The fiddler made a squeak on two notes that sounded like *kiss-her*, and from a corner of the booth there came a clamorous smack of lips.

'I saw you sweetheartin' laal Bessy,' said one of the fellows to another.

'And I saw *you* last night cutteran sa

soft in the meadow. Nay, dunnot look sa strange. I never say nowt, not I. Only yon mother of Aggy's, she's a famous fratcher, and dunnot you let *her* get wind. She brays the lasses, and mappen she'll bray somebody forby.'

While the dancing proceeded there was a noisy clatter of glasses, and a mutter of voices in the neighbourhood of the bar.

'The varra crony one's fidgin to see. Gie us a shak' of thy daddle,' shouted a fellow with a face like a russet apple.

'Come, Dick, let's bottom a quart together. Deil tak' the expense.'

'Why, man, and wherever hasta been since Whissen Monday?'

'Weel, you see, I went to the fair and stood with a straw in my mouth, and the wives all came round, and one of them sayd, "What wage do you ask, canny lad?" "Five pound ten," I says. "And what can you do?" she says. "Do?" I says, "anything from ploughing to threshing and nicking a nag's tail," I says. "Come, be my man," she says. But she was like to clem me, so I packed up my bits of duds and got my wage in my reet-hand breek pocket, and here I am.'

The dancing had finished, and a little group was gathered around the fiddler's tub.

'Come thy ways; here's Tom o' Dint conjuring, and telling folk what they are thinking.'

'That's mair nor he could do for the numskulls as never think.'

'He bangs all the player-folk, does Tom.'

'Who's yon tatterdemalion flinging by the newspaper and bawling, "The country's going to the dogs"?'

'That's Grey Graham, setting folk by the lug with his blusteration.'

'Mess, lads, but he'd be a reet good Parli'ment man to threep about the nation.'

'Weel, I's na pollytishin, but if it's tearin' and snappin' same as a terrier that mak's a reet good Parli'ment man, I reckon not all England could bang him.'

'And that's not saying nowt, Sim. I've heard Grey Graham on the ballot till it's wet him through to the waistcoat.'

'Is that Mister Paul Ritson and Mistress Lowther just run in for shelter?'

'Surely, and a reet bonny lass she is.'

'And he's got larnin' and manners too.'

'Ey, he's of the bettermer sort is Paul.'

'Does she live at the parson's—Parson Christian's?'

'Why, yes, man, it's only naturable— he's her guardian.'

'And what a man he is to be sure.'

'Ey, we'll never see his like again when he's gone.'

'Nay, not till water runs up bank and trees grow down bank.'

' And what a scholar, and no pride neither, and what's mair in a parson, no greed. Why, the leal fellow values the world and the world's gear not a flea.'

' Contentment's a kingdom, as folk say, and religion is no worse for a bit o' charity.'

There was a momentary pressure of the company towards the mouth of the booth, where Gubblum Oglethorpe reappeared with his pack swung from his neck in front of him. The girls gathered eagerly around.

' What have you to-day, Gubblum ?'

' Nay, nowt for you, my dear. You're one of them that allus looks best with nothing on.'

' Oh, Gubblum !'

The compliment was certainly a dubious one.

' Only your bits of shabby duds—that's all that pretty faces like yours wants.'

' Oh Gubblum !'

The pedlar was evidently a dear simple soul.

'Lord bless you, yes; what's in here,' slapping his pack contemptuously, 'it's only for them wizzent old creatures up in London —them 'at have faces like the map of England when it shows all the lines of the railways—just to make them a bit presentable, you know. And there is no knowing what some of these things won't do to mak' a body smart—what with brooches and handkerchers and collars, and *I* don't know what.'

Gubblum's air of indifference had the extraordinary effect of bringing a dozen pairs of gloating eyes on the strapped pack. The face of the pedlar wore an expression of bland innocence as he continued :

'But bless you, I'm such a straight-forrard chap, or I'd make my fortune with the like of what's here.'

'Open your pack, Gubblum,' said one of

the fellows, Geordie Moore, prompted by
sundry prods from the elbow of a little
damsel by his side.

The ' straightforrard chap' made a depre-
catory gesture, and then yielded obligingly.
While loosening the straps he resumed his
discourse on his own general ignorance of
business tactics, his ruinous honesty and
demoralizing sense of honour.

' I'm not cute enough, that's my fault.
I know the way to my mouth with a
spoonful of poddish, and that's all.   If I go
farther in the dark I'm lost.'

Gubblum opened his pack and drew forth
a gaudy red and green shawl of a hideous
pattern.

' Now, just to give you a sample.   Here's
a nice neat shawl that I never had no more
nor two of.   Well, I actually sold the
fellow of that shawl for seven-and-
sixpence !'

The look of amazement at his own

shortcomings which sat on the childlike face of the pedlar was answered by the expression of mock surprise in the face of Paul Ritson, who came up at the moment, took the shawl from Gubblum's outstretched arms, and said in a hushed whisper:

'No, did you now!'

Geordie Moore thereupon dived into his pocket, and brought out three half-crowns.

'Here's for you, Gubblum; let's have it.'

''Od bliss me,' cried the elderly cynic, 'but that Gubblum will never mak' his plack a bawbee.'

And Grey Graham, having disposed of the affairs of the nation and witnessed Geordie's snap at the pedlar's bait, cried out in a bitter laugh:

'"There's little wit within his powe
That lights a candle at the lowe."'

Just then a tumult arose in the vicinity

of the bar. The two cronies were at open war.

'Deuce take it, I had fifteen white shillin' in my reet-hand breek pocket, and where are they now?'

''Od dang thee, what should I know about your brass? You're kicking up a stour to waken a corp.'

'I had fifteen white shillin' in my reet-hand breek pocket, I tell thee.'

'What's that to me, thou poor shaffles? You're as drunk as muck. Do you think I've taken your brass? You've got a wrong pig by the lug if you reckon to come ower me.'

'They were in my reet-hand breek pocket, I'll swear on it.'

'What a fratchin—try your left-hand breek pocket.'

The russet-faced ploughman thrust his hand where directed, and instantly a comical smile of mingled joy and shame overspread his countenance. There was a gurgling laugh, through which the voice of the pedlar could be heard saying :

‘ We’ll mak’ thee King ower the cockers, my canny lad.’

The canny lad was slinking away amid a derisive titter when a great silence fell on the booth. Those in front fell back, and those behind craned their necks to see over the heads of the people before them.

At the mouth of the booth stood the old Laird Fisher, his face ghastly pale, his eyes big and restless, the rain dripping from his long hair and beard.

‘ They’ve telt me,’ he began in a strange voice, ‘ they’ve telt me that my Mercy has gone off in the London train. I reckon they’re mistook as to the lass, but I’ve come to see for mysel’. Is she here ?’

None answered. Only the heavy rain-drops that pattered on the canvas overhead broke the silence. Paul Ritson pushed his way through the crowd.

'Mercy?—London?—Wait, Matthew; I'll see if she's here.'

The Laird Fisher looked from face to face of the people about him.

'Any on you know owt about her?' he asked in a low voice. 'Why don't. you speak, some on you? You shake your heads—what does that mean?'

The old man was struggling to control the emotion that was surging in his throat.

'No, Matthew, she's not here,' said Paul Ritson.

'Then maybe it's true,' said Matthew, with a strange quiet.

There was a pause. Paul was the first to shake off his surprise.

'She might be at Little Town — in Keswick—twenty places.'

'She *might* be, Master Paul, but she's

nowt o' the sort. She's on her way to London, Mercy is !'

It was Natt, the stableman at the Ghyll, who spoke.

At that the old man's trance seemed to break.

' Gone ? Mercy gone ? Gone without a word ? Why ? Where ?'

' She'd her little red bundle aside her ; and she cried a gay bit to hersel' in the corner. I saw her mysel'.'

Paul's face became rigid with anger.

' There's villainy in this——be sure of that,' he said hotly.

The Laird rocked his head backwards and forwards, and his eyes swam with tears ; but he stood in the middle as quiet as a child.

' My laal Mercy,' he said faintly, ' gone from her old father.'

Paul stepped to the old man's side, and put a great hand on his shoulder as softly

as a woman might have soothed her babe.
Then turning about, and glancing wrathfully
in the faces around them, he said :

'Some waistrel has been at work here.
Who is he ? Speak out. Anybody know ?'

No one spoke. Only the Laird moaned
feebly, and reeled like a drunken man.
Then, with the first shock over, the old
man began to laugh. What a laugh it
was !

'No matter!' he said; 'no matter! Now
I've nowt left I've nowt to lose. There's
comfort in that, anyways! Ha, ha, ha!
But my heart is like to choke for all. You
say reet, Mr. Ritson, there's villainy in it.'

The old man's eyes wandered vacantly.

'Her own father,' he mumbled ; 'her
lone old father—broken-hearted—him 'at
loved her—no matter, I've nowt left to—
Ha, ha, ha !'

He tried to walk away jauntily, and with
a ghastly smile on his battered face, but he

stumbled and fell insensible into Paul's outstretched arms. They loosened his necker-
chief and bathed his forehead.

Just then Hugh Ritson strode into the
tent, stepped up to the group, and looked
down over the bent heads at the stricken
father lying in his brother's arms.

Paul's lips trembled and his powerful
frame quivered.

' Who knows but the scoundrel is here
now,' he said ; and his eyes traversed the
men about him. ' If he is, let him look at
his pitiless work ; and may the sight follow
him to his death !'

At that moment Hugh Ritson's face
underwent an awful change. Then the old
man opened his eyes in consciousness, and
Hugh knelt before him and put a glass of
water to his lips.

In the homestead of the Ritsons the wide old ingle was aglow with a cheerful fire, and Mrs. Ritson stood before it baking oaten cake on a 'girdle.' The table was laid for supper with beef and beer and milk and barley-bread. In the seat of a recessed window, Paul Ritson and Greta Lowther sat together.

At intervals that grew shorter, and with a grave face that became more anxious, Mrs. Ritson walked to the door and looked out into the thickening sky. The young people had been too much absorbed to notice her increasing perturbation, until she opened a clothes chest and took out dry

flannels and spread them on the hearth to
air.

'Don't worrit yourself, mother,' said
Paul. 'He'll be here soon. He had to
cross the Coledale Pass, and that's a long
stroke of the ground, you know.'

'It's an hour past supper-time,' said
Mrs. Ritson, glancing aside at the old clock
that ticked audibly from behind the great
arm-chair. 'The rain is coming again—
listen!' There was a light patter of rain-
drops against the window-panes. 'If
he's on the fells now he'll be wet to the
skin.'

'I wish I'd gone in place of him,' said
Paul, turning to Greta. 'A bad wetting
troubles him nowadays! Not same as of
old, when he'd follow the fells all day long
knee-deep in water and soaked to the skin
with rain or snow!'

A thunder-clap shook the house. The
windows rattled, and the lamp that had

been newly lit and put on the table flickered slightly and burnt red.

'Mercy me, what a night! Was that a flash of lightning?' said Mrs. Ritson, and she walked to the door once more and opened it.

'Don't worrit, mother!' repeated Paul. 'Do come in. Father will be here soon, and if he gets a wetting there's no help for it now.'

Paul had turned aside from an animated conversation with Greta to interpolate this remonstrance against his mother's anxiety. Resuming the narrative of his exciting wrestling match, he described its thrilling incidents as much by gesture as by words.

'John Proudfoot took me—so—and tried to give me the cross-buttock, but I caught his eye and twisted him on my hip—so—and down he went in a bash!'

A hurried knock came to the outer door.

In an instant it was opened, and a white face looked in.

'What's now, Reuben?' said Paul, rising to his feet.

'Come along with me—leave the women-folk behind—master's down—the lightning has struck him—I'm afeart he's dead.'

'My father!' said Paul, and stood for a moment with a bewildered look. 'Go on, Reuben, I'll follow.' Paul picked up his hat and was gone in an instant.

Mrs. Ritson had been stooping over the griddle when Reuben entered. She heard what he said, and rose up with a face of deadly pallor. But she said nothing, and sank helplessly into a chair. Then Greta stepped up to her and kissed her.

'Mother—dear mother!' she said, and Mrs. Ritson dropped her head on the girl's breast.

Hugh had been sitting over some papers in his own room off the first landing. He overheard the announcement, and came into the hall.

'Your father has been struck by the lightning,' said Greta.

'They will fetch him home,' said Hugh.

At the next moment there was the sound from without of burdened footsteps. They were bearing the injured man. Through the back of the house they carried him to his room.

'That is for my sake,' said Mrs. Ritson, raising her tear-stained face to listen.

Paul entered. His ruddy cheeks had grown ashy white. His eyes, that had blinked with pleasure a minute ago, now stared wide with fear.

'Is he alive?'

'Yes.'

'Thank God! oh, thank God for ever and ever! Let me go in to him.'

'He is unconscious—he breathes—but no more.'

Mrs. Ritson, with Paul and Greta, went into the room in which they had placed the stricken man. He lay across the bed in his clothes, just as he had fallen. They bathed his forehead and applied leeches to his temples. He breathed heavily, but gave no sign of consciousness.

Paul sat at his father's side with his face buried in his hands. He was recalling his boyish days, when his father would lift him in his arms and throw him on the bare back of the pony that he gave him on his thirteenth birthday. Could it be possible that the end was at hand!

He got up and led Greta out of the room.

' This house of mourning is no place for you,' he said; ' the storm is over : you must leave us; Natt can put the mare into the trap and drive you home.'

' I shall not go,' said Greta; ' this shall be my home to-night. Don't send me away from you, Paul. You are in trouble, and my place is here.'

' You could do no good, and might take some harm.'

Mrs. Ritson came out.

' Where is Mr. Bonnithorne?' she asked. ' He was to be here at eight. Your father might recover consciousness.'

' The lawyer could do nothing to help him.'

' If he is to leave us, may it please God to give him one little hour of conscious-ness.'

' Yes, knowing us again—giving us a farewell word.'

' There is another reason—a more ter-rible reason.'

' You are thinking of the will. Let that go by. Come, mother—and Greta, too— come, let us go back.'

Half an hour later the house was as still as the chamber of death. With hushed

voices and noiseless steps the women-
servants moved to and from the room
where lay the dying man. The farming
men sat together in an outer kitchen, and
talked in whispers.

The storm had passed away; the stars
struggled one by one through a rack of
flying cloud, and a silver fringe of moonlight sometimes fretted the black patches of
the sky.

Hugh Ritson sat alone in the old hall,
that was now desolate enough. His face
rested on his hand, and his elbow on his
knee. There was a strange light in his
eyes. It was not sorrow, and it was not
joy; it was anxiety, uncertainty, perturbation. Again and again he started up from
a deep reverie, and then a half-smothered
cry escaped him. He walked a few paces
to and fro, and sat down once more.

A servant crossed the hall on tiptoe.
Hugh raised his head.

'How is your patient now?' he said quietly.

'Just breathing, sir; still quite unconscious.'

Hugh got up uneasily. A mirror hung on the wall in front of him, and he stood and looked vacantly into it. His thoughts wandered, and when a gleam of consciousness returned the first object that he saw was the reflection of his own face. It was full of light and expression. Perhaps it wore a ghostly smile. He turned away from the sight impatiently.

Sitting down again he tried to compose himself. Point by point he revolved the situation. He thought of what the lawyer had said of the deserted wife and lost son of Lowther. Then, taking out of an inner pocket the medallion that Mr. Bonnithorne had lent him, he looked at it long and earnestly.

The inspection seemed to afford a grim

satisfaction.   There could be no doubt now
of the ghostly smile that played upon his
face.

There was a tall antique clock in the
corner of the hall.   It struck eight.   The
slow beats of the bell echoed chillily in the
hushed apartment.   The hour awakened
the consciousness of the brooding man.
At eight o'clock Mr. Bonnithorne was ap-
pointed to be there to make the will.

Hugh Ritson touched gently a handbell
that   stood   on   the   table.   A   servant
entered.

' Send Natt to me,' said Hugh.

A moment later the stableman shambled
into the hall.   He was a thick-set young
fellow with a short neck and a full face,
and eyelids that hung deep over a pair of
cunning eyes.   At first sight one would
have said that the rascal was only half
awake; at the second glance, that he was
never asleep.

Hugh received him with a show of cordiality.

'Ah, Natt, come here—closer.'

The man walked across. Hugh dropped his voice.

'Go down to Little Town and find Mr. Bonnithorne. You may meet him on the way. If not, he will be at the Flying Horse. Tell him *I* sent you to say that Adam Fallow lies dying at Bigrigg, and must see him at once. You understand?'

The man lifted his slumbrous eyelids. A suspicious twinkle lurked beneath them. He glanced around, then down at his big, grimy boots, measured with one uplifted hand the altitude of the bump on the top of his bullet head, and muttered, '*I* understand.'

Hugh's face darkened.

'Silence,' he said sternly, and then he met Natt's upward glance with a faint smile.

' When you come back, get yourself out of the way—do you hear ?'

The heavy eyelids went up once more. ' *I* hear.'

' Then be off.'

The fellow was shuffling away.

' Natt,' said Hugh, following him a step, ' you fancied that new whip of mine ; take it. You'll find it in the porch.'

A smile crossed Natt's face from ear to ear. He stumbled out.

Hugh Ritson returned to the hearth. That haunting mirror caught the light of his eyes again and showed him that he too was smiling. At the same instant there came from the inner room the dull dead sound of a deep sob. It banished the smile and made him pause. He looked at the reflection of his face—could it be the face of a scoundrel ? Was he playing a base part ? No, he was merely asserting his rights ; his plain legal rights—nothing more.

He opened a cupboard in the wall and took down a bunch of keys. Selecting one key, he stepped up to a cabinet and opened it. In a compartment were many loose papers. Now to see if by chance there existed a will already. He glanced at the papers one by one and threw them aside. When he had finished his inspection he took a hasty turn about the room. No trace—he had been sure of it!

Again the deep sob came from within. Hugh Ritson walked noiselessly to the inner door, opened it slightly, bent his head and listened. He turned away with an expression of pain, picked up his hat and went out.

The night was very dark. He strode a few paces down the lonnin and then back to the porch. Uncovering his head he let the night wind cool his hot temples. His breath came audibly and hard. He was turning again into the house when his eye was arrested by a light near the turning of the high-road. The light was approaching; he walked towards it, and met Josiah Bonnithorne. The lawyer was jouncing along towards the house with a lantern in his hand.

'Didn't you meet the stableman?' said Hugh in an eager whisper.

'No.'

'The blockhead must have taken the old pack-horse road on the fell side. One would be safe in that fool's stupidity. You have heard what has happened?'

'I have. Fortune falls into your hand.'

'There is no will already, Bonnithorne.'

'And your father is insensible?'

'Yes.'

'Then none shall be made.'

There was a pause, in which the darkness itself seemed full of speech. The lantern cast its light only on an open cart-shed in the lane.

'If your mother is the Grace Ormerod who married Robert Lowther and had a son by him, then Paul was that son—the heir of Lowther's conscience-money.'

'Bonnithorne,' said Hugh Ritson—his voice trembled and broke, 'if it is so, then it *is* so, and *we* need do nothing. Remember, he is my father. It is not within belief that he wants to disinherit his own son for the son of another man.'

Mr. Bonnithorne broke into a half-smothered laugh, and stepped close into the cobble-hedge, keeping the lantern down.

'Your father—yes! But you have seen to-day what that may come to. He has always held you under his hand. Paul has been the old man's favourite.'

'No doubt of that.' Hugh crept close to the lawyer. He was wrestling in the coil of a tragic temptation.

'If he recovers consciousness, he **may**

be tempted to recognise as his own his wife's illegitimate son. *That*'—the low tone was one of withering irony—'will keep her from dishonour, and you from the estates.'

'At least he is my brother, Bonnithorne —my mother's son. If my father wishes to provide for him, God forbid that we should prevent.'

Once more the half-smothered laugh came through the darkness.

'You have missed your vocation, Mr. Ritson. Believe me, the Gospel has lost a fervent advocate. Odd, isn't it? Perhaps you would like to pray for this good brother: perhaps you would consider it *safe* to drop to your knee and say, "My good brother that should be, who has ever loved me, whom I have ever loved, take here my fortune and leave me until death a penniless dependent on the lands that are mine by right of birth." '

Hugh Ritson's breath came in gusts through his quivering, unseen lips.

'Bonnithorne, it cannot be—it is mere coincidence, seductive damning coincidence. My mother knows all. If it were true that Paul was the son of Lowther, she would know that Paul and Greta must be half-brother and half-sister. She would stop their unnatural union.'

'And do you think I have waited until now to sound that shoal water with a cautious plummet? Your mother is as ignorant of the propinquity as Greta herself. Lowther was dead before your family settled in Newlands. The families never once came together while the widow lived. And now not a relative survives who can tell the story.'

'Parson Christian?' said Hugh Ritson.

'Pshaw! A great child just out of swaddling-clothes.'

' Then the secret rests with me and you, Bonnithorne ?'

' Who else ? The marriage must not come off.   Greta is Paul's half-sister, but she is no relative of *yours*——'

' You are right, Bonnithorne,' Hugh Ritson broke in ; ' the marriage is against nature.'

' And the first step towards stopping it is to stop the will.'

' Then why are you here ?'

' To make sure that there is no will already.   You have satisfied me, and now I go.'

There was a pause.

' Who shall say that I am acting a base part ?' said Hugh in an eager tone.

' Who indeed ?'

' Nature itself is on my side.'

The man was conquered.   He was in the grip of his temptation.

' I am off, Mr. Ritson.   Get back into

the house. It is not *safe* for you to be out of sight and sound.'

Mr. Bonnithorne was moving off in the darkness, the lamp before his breast; its light for that instant on Hugh Ritson's haggard face.

' Wait; put out your lamp.'

' It's done.'

All was now dark.

' Good-night.'

' Good-night.'

With slow whispers the two men parted.

The springy step of Josiah Bonnithorne was soon lost in the road below.

Hugh Ritson stood for a while where the lawyer left him, and then turned back into the house. He found the cabinet open. In the turmoil of emotion he had forgotten to close it. He returned to it, and shuffled with the papers to put them back in their place. At that moment the door opened, and a heavy footstep fell on the floor. Hugh glanced up startled. It was Paul. His face was ploughed deep with lines of pain. But the cloud of sorrow that it wore was not so black as the cloud of anger when he saw what his brother was doing and guessed his purpose.

'What are you about?' Paul asked, mastering his wrath.

There was no response.

'What devil's work are you doing now —here—and in an hour like this?'

Still no response.

'Shut up that cabinet.'

Hugh turned about with a flushed face.

'I shall do as I please.'

Paul took two strides towards him.

'Shut it up.'

The cabinet was closed. At the same moment Mrs. Ritson came from the inner room. Paul turned on his heel.

'He is thinking of the will,' said the elder brother. 'Perhaps it is natural that he should distrust me, but when the time comes he is welcome to the half of everything, and ten thousand wills would hardly give him more.'

Mrs. Ritson was strongly agitated. Her eyes, red with weeping, were aflame with expression.

'Paul, he is conscious,' she cried, in a voice that her anxiety could not subdue. 'He is trying to speak. Where is the lawyer?'

Hugh had been moving towards the outer door.

'Conscious!' he repeated, and returned to the hearth.

'Send for Mr. Bonnithorne at once,' said Mrs. Ritson, addressing Hugh.

Her manner was feverish. Hugh touched the bell. When the servant appeared he said:

'Tell Natt to run to the village for Mr. Bonnithorne.'

Paul had walked to the door of the inner room. His hand was on the handle, when the door opened and Greta came out. She stepped up to Mrs. Ritson and tried to quiet her agitation.

The servant returned.

'I can't find Natt,' she said. 'He is not in the house.'

'You'll find him in the stable,' said Hugh composedly.

The servant went out hurriedly.

Paul returned to the middle of the room.

'I'll go myself,' he said, and plucked up his hat from the settle, but Mrs. Ritson rose to prevent him.

'No, no, Paul,' she said in a tremulous voice, '*you* must never leave his side.'

Paul glanced at his brother with a perplexed look. The calmness of Hugh's manner disturbed him.

The servant re-appeared.

'Natt is not in the stable, sir.'

Paul's face was growing crimson. Mrs. Ritson turned to Hugh.

'Hugh, my dear son, do you go for the lawyer.'

A faint smile that lurked at the corners of Hugh's mouth gave way to a look of grievous injury.

'Mother, *my* place, also, is here. How can you ask me to leave my father's side at a moment like this?'

Greta had been looking fixedly at Hugh.

'I'll go,' she said resolutely.

'Impossible,' said Paul. 'It is now dark—the roads are wet and lonely.'

'I'll go, nevertheless,' said Greta firmly.

'God bless you, my darling, and love you and keep you for ever and ever,' said Paul. Wrapping a cloak about her shoulders he whispered, 'My brave girl— that's the stuff of which an Englishwoman may be made.'

He opened the door and walked out with

her across the courtyard. The night was
now clear and calm ; the stars burnt ; the
trees whispered ; the distant ghylls, swollen
by the rain, roared loud through the thin
air ; a bird on the bough of a fir-tree
whistled and chirped. The storm was
gone ; only its wreckage lay in the still
room within.

'A safe journey to you, dear girl, and a
speedy return,' whispered Paul, and in
another moment Greta had vanished in
the gloom.

When he returned to the hall, his brother
was passing into the room where the sick
man lay. Paul was about to follow, when
his mother, who was walking aimlessly to
and fro in yet more violent agitation than
before, called on him to remain. He turned
about and stepped up to her, observing,
as he did so, that Hugh had paused on the
threshold, and was regarding them with a
steadfast look.

Mrs. Ritson took Paul's hand with a nervous grasp. Her eyes, that bore the marks of recent tears, had the light of wild excitement.

'God be praised that he is conscious at last,' she said.

Paul shook his head as if in censure of his mother's feelings.

'Let him die in peace,' he said; 'let his soul pass quietly to its rest. Don't vex it now with thoughts of the cares it leaves behind.'

Mrs. Ritson let go his hand, and dropped into a chair. A slight shudder passed over her. Paul looked down with a puzzled expression. Then there was a low sobbing. He leaned over his mother and smoothed her hair tenderly.

'Come, let us go in,' he said in a broken voice.

Mrs. Ritson rose from her seat and went down on her knees. Her eyes, still wet, but no longer weeping, were raised to heaven.

'Almighty Father, give me strength!' she said beneath her breath, and then more quietly she rose to her feet.

Paul regarded her with increasing perturbation. Something even more serious than he yet knew of was amiss. Hardly knowing why, his heart sank still deeper.

'What are we doing?' he said, scarcely realizing his own words.

Mrs. Ritson threw herself on his neck.

'Did I not say there was a terrible reason why your father should make a will?'

Paul's voice seemed to die within him.

'What is it, mother?' he asked feebly, not yet gathering the meaning of his fears.

'God knows, I never dreamt it would be my lips that must tell you,' said Mrs. Ritson.

' Paul, my son, my darling son, you think me a good mother and a pure woman. I am neither. I must confess all—now— and to you. Oh, how your love will turn from me ! How you will hate me ! How every kiss I have given you will seem to leave blisters on your lips !'

Paul's face turned pale. His eyes gazed into his mother's eyes with a fixed look. The clock ticked audibly. Not another sound broke the silence. At last Paul spoke.

' Speak, mother,' he said ; ' is it something about my father ?'

Mrs. Ritson's face fell on to her son's breast. A strong shudder ran over her shoulders, and she sobbed aloud.

' You are not your father's heir,' she said ; ' you were born before we married. . . . . But you will try not to hate me, . . your own mother. . . . You will try, will you not ?'

Paul's great frame shook visibly. He tried to speak. His tongue clave to his mouth.

'Do you mean that I am——a bastard,' he said in a hoarse whisper.

The word seemed to sting his mother like a poisoned arrow She clung yet closer about his neck.

'Pity me and love me still, though I have wronged you before God and man—I whom the world thought so pure—I am but a whited sepulchre—a dishonoured woman dishonouring her dearest son.'

The door opened gently, and Hugh Ritson stood in the doorway. Neither his brother nor his mother realized his presence. He remained a moment, and then withdrew, leaving the door ajar.

Beneath the two whom he left behind the world at that moment reeled.

Paul stood with great, wide eyes, that had never tear to soften them, gazing vacantly into the weeping eyes before him. His lips quivered, but he did not speak.

'Paul, speak to me—speak to me—only speak—curse me, yes, curse me, if you will—only let me hear your voice ! See, I am at your feet—your mother kneels to you—forgive her as God has forgiven her.'

And loosing her grasp, she flung herself on the ground before him, and covered her face with her hands.

Paul seemed not at first to know what was happening. Then he stooped and raised his mother to her feet.

'Mother, rise up,' he said in a strange, hollow tone. 'Who am I that I should presume to pardon you ? I am your son—you are my mother.'

His vacant eyes gathered a startled expression. He glanced quickly around the room, and said in a deep whisper :

'How many know of this ?'

'None beside ourselves.'

The frightened look disappeared. In its place came a look of overwhelming agony.

'But *I* know of it ; oh, my God !' he cried ; and into the chair from which his mother had risen he fell like a wounded man.

Mrs. Ritson dried her eyes. A strange quiet was coming upon her now. Her voice gathered strength. She laid a hand on the hand of her son, who sat before her with buried face.

'Paul,' she said, ' it is not until now that the day of reckoning has waited for *me*. When you were a babe, and knew nothing of your mother's grief, I sorrowed over the shame that might yet be yours ; and when you grew to be a prattling child I thought if God would look into your innocent eyes they would purchase grace for both of us.'

Paul lifted his head. At that moment of distress God had sent him the gracious gift of tears. His eyes were wet, and looked tenderly at his mother.

'Paul,' she continued, quite calmly now, 'promise me one thing.'

'What is it?' he asked softly.

'That if your father should not live to make the will that must recognise you as his son, you will never reveal this secret.'

Paul rose to his feet. 'That is impossible. I cannot promise it,' he said.

'Why?'

'Honour and justice require that my brother Hugh, and not I, should be my father's heir—he, at least, must know.'

'What honour, and what justice?'

'The honour of a true man—the justice of the law of England.'

Mrs. Ritson dropped her head. 'So much for *your* honour,' she said. 'But what of *mine?*'

'Mother, what do you mean?'

'That if you allow your younger brother

to inherit, the world by that act will be told all—your father's sin, your mother's shame.'

Mrs. Ritson raised her hands to her face, and turned aside. Paul stepped up to her and kissed her forehead reverently.

'You are right,' he said. 'Forgive me —I thought only of myself. The world that loves to tarnish a pure name would like to gloat over your sorrow. That it shall never! Man's law may have been outraged, but God's law is still inviolate. Whatever my birth, I am as much your son in the light of Heaven as Jacob was the son of Isaac, or David of Jesse. Come, let us go in to him—he may yet live to acknowledge me.'

It had been a terrible moment, but it was past. To live to manhood in ignorance of the dishonour of his birth, and then to learn the truth under the shadow of death—this had been a tragic experience. The love he

had borne his father—the reverence he had
learnt at his mother's knee—to what bitter
test had they there been put! Had all the
past been but as the marble image of a
happy life! Was all the future shattered
before him! Pshaw! he was the unconscious slave of a superstition—a phantasm,
a gingerbread superstition!

And a mightier touch awoke his sensibilities—the touch of nature. Before God
at that moment he was his father's son. If
the world, or the world's law, said other-
wise, then they were of the devil, and
deserving to be damned. What rite, what
jabbering ceremony, what priestly ordinance,
what legal mummery, stood between him
and his claim to his father's name?

Paul took in love the hand of his mother.
'Let us go in to him,' he repeated, and
together they walked across the room.

The outer door was flung open, and
Greta entered, flushed and with wide-open

eyes.   At the same instant the inner door
swung noiselessly back, and Hugh Ritson
stood on the threshold.   Greta was about
to speak, but Hugh motioned her to silence.
His face was pale, his hand trembled.   ' Too
late,' he said huskily, ' he is dead.'

Greta sank on to the settle in the window
recess.   Hugh walked to the hearth and
paused with rigid features before the haunting mirror.

Paul stood for a moment hand-in-hand
with his mother, motionless, speechless,
cold at his heart.   Then he hurried into
the inner room.   Mrs. Ritson followed him,
closing the door behind her.

The little oak-bound room was dusky ;
the lamp that burnt low was shaded.
Across the bed lay Allan Ritson, in his
habit as he lived.   But his lips were white
and cold.

Paul stood and looked down.   There lay
his father—his father still !   His father by

right of nature—of love—of honour—let the world say what it would.

And he knew the truth at last: too late to look into those glassy eyes and read the secret of their long years of suffering love.

'Father,' Paul whispered, and fell to his knees by the deaf ear.

Mrs. Ritson, strangely quiet, strangely calm, stepped to the opposite side of the bed, and placed one hand on the dead man's breast.

'Paul,' she said, 'come here.'

He rose to his feet and walked to her side.

'Lay your hand with mine, and pledge to me your solemn word never to speak of what you have heard to-night until that great day when we three shall stand together before the great white throne.'

Paul placed his hand side by side with hers, and lifted his eyes to heaven.

'On my father's body, by my mother's honour—never to reveal to any human soul, by word or deed, his act or her shame—always to bear myself as their lawful son before man, even as I am their rightful son before God—I swear it! I swear it!'

His voice was cold and clear, but the words were scarcely uttered when he fell to his knees again, with a subdued cry of overwrought feeling.

Mrs. Ritson staggered back, caught the curtains of the bed, and covered her face. All was still.

Then a shuffling footfall was heard on the floor. Hugh Ritson was in the darkened room. He lifted the shaded lamp from the table, approached the bedside, and held the lamp with one hand above his head. The light fell on the outstretched body of his father and the bowed head of his brother.

BOOK SECOND.

THE COIL OF THE TEMPTATION.

CHAPTER I.

It was late in November, and the day was dark and drear. Hoar-frost lay on the ground. The atmosphere was pallid with haze and dense with mystery. Gaunt spectres of white mist swept across the valley and gathered at the sides of every open door. The mountains were gone. Only a fibrous vagueness was visible.

In an old pasture field by the bridge, a man was ploughing. He was an elderly man, sturdy and stolid of figure, and clad in blue homespun. There was nothing clerical in his garb or manner, yet he was the vicar and schoolmaster of the parish. His low-crowned hat was drawn deep over his slumberous grey eyes. The mobile mouth beneath completed the expression of gentleness and easy good-nature. It was a fine old face, with the beauty of simplicity and the sweetness of content.

A boy in front led the horses and whistled. The parson hummed a tune as he turned his furrows. Sometimes he sang in a drawling tone—

‘ Bonny lass, canny lass, wilta be mine ?
Thou’s nowder wesh dishes nor sarra the swine.’

At the turn-rows he paused, and rested on his plough handles. He rested longest at the turn-rows on the road side of the field. Like the shivering mists that grouped about the open doors, he was held there by light and warmth.

The smithy stood at the opposite side of the road, cut into the rock of the fell on three sides, and having a roof of thatch. The glare of the fire, now rising, now falling, streamed through the open door. It sent a long vista of light through the blank and pulsating haze. The vibrations of the anvil were all but the only sounds on the air; the alternate thin clink of the smith's hand hammer and the thick thud of the striker's sledge echoed in unseen recesses of the hills beyond.

This smithy of Newland filled the function which under a higher propitiousness of circumstances is answered by a club. Girded with his leather apron, his sleeves rolled tightly over his knotty arms, the smith, John Proudfoot, stood waiting for his heat. His striker, Geordie Moore, had fallen to at the bellows. On the tool chest sat Gubblum Oglethorpe, leisurely smoking. His pony was tied to the hasp of the gate. The miller, Dick of the Syke, sat on a pile of iron rods. Tom o' Dint, the little bow-legged fiddler and postman, was sharpening at the grindstone a pen-

knife already worn obliquely to a point by
many similar applications.

'Nay, I can make nowt of him. He's
a changed man for sure,' said the blacksmith.

Gubblum removed his pipe and muttered
sententiously, 'It's die-spensy, I tell thee.'

'Dandering and wandering about at all
hours of the day and night,' continued the
blacksmith.

'It's all die-spensy,' repeated the pedlar.

'And as widderful and wizzent as a pole-
cat nailed up on a barn door,' said Tom o'
Dint, lifting his grating knife from the
grindstone and speaking with a voice as
hoarse.

'Ey, and as weak as watter with it,'
added the blacksmith.

'Him as was as strong as rum punch,'
rejoined the fiddler.

'It's die-spensy, John—nowt else,' said
Gubblum.

The miller broke in testily. 'What's die-spensy?'

'What ails Paul Ritson,' answered Gubblum.

'Shaf on your balderdash,' said Dick of the Syke; 'die-spensying and die-spensying. You've no'but your die-spensy for everything. Tommy's rusty throat, and John's big toe, and lang Geordie's broken nose, as Giles Raisley gave him a' Saturday neet at the Pack Horse—it's all die-spensy.'

The miller was a blusterous fellow, who could swear in lusty anger and laugh in boisterous sport in a single breath.

Gubblum puffed placidly. 'It *is* die-spensy. I know it by exper'ence,' he observed persistently.

The blacksmith's little eyes twinkled mischievously. 'To be sure you do, Gubblum. You had it bad the day you crossed in the packet from Whitchebben. That was die-spensy— a 'cute bout too.'

'I've heard as it were amazing rough on the watter that day,' said Tom in a pause of the wheel, glancing up knowingly at the blacksmith.

'*Heard*, have you? Must have been tolerable deaf else. *Rough?* Why, they do say as the packet were wrecked, and only two planks saved. Gubblum was washed ashore cross-legged on one of them, and his pack on the other.'

The long laboured breathings of the bellows ended, the iron was thrown white hot out of the glowing coals on to the anvil, and the clank of the hand hammer and thud of the sledge were all that could be heard. Then the iron cooled, and was lifted back into the palpitating blaze. The blacksmith stepped to the door, wiped his streaming forehead with one hand and waved the other to the parson ploughing in the opposite field. 'A canny morning, Mr. Christian,' he shouted. 'Bad luck for the parson's young lady, anyhow—her sweetheart is none too keen for the wedding,' he said, turning again to the fire.

'She's a fine like lass, yon,' said Tom o' Dint.

An old man, iron grey, with a pair of mason's mallets swung front and back across his shoulders, stepped into the smithy. 'How fend ye, John?' he said.

'Middling weel, Job,' answered the blacksmith; 'and what's your errand now?'

'A chisel or two for tempering.'

'Cutting in the churchyard to-day, Job? Cold wark, eh?'

'Ey, auld Ritson's stone as they've putten over him.'

The blacksmith tapped the pedlar on the arm. 'Gubblum, shall I tell you what's a-matter with Paul?'

'Never you bother, John, it's die-spensy.'

' It's fretting—that's it—fretting for his father.'

'Fretting for his fiddlesticks!' shouted Dick, the miller; 'Allan's dead this half a year.'

' John's reet,' said Job, the stonecutter; ' it *is* fretting.'

Dick of the Syke got up off the iron rods. ' Because a young fellow has given you a job of wark to cut his father's headstone and tell a lie or two in letters half an inch deep and two shillings a dozen—does that show 'at he's fretting ?'

' He didn't do nowt of the sort,' said Job hotly.

' Dusta mean as it were the other one-— Hugh ?' inquired the miller.

' Maybe tha's reet,' said Job.

Dick of the Syke was not to be beaten for lack of the logic of circumlocution.

' Then what for do you say as Paul is weeping his insides out about his father, when he leaves it to other folks to put a bit of a stone over him and a few scrats on it ?'

'Because I do say so,' said Job conclusively.

'And maybe you've got your reasons, Job,' said the blacksmith with insinuating suavity.

'Maybe I have,' said the mason. Then softening, he added, 'I don't mind telling you, neither. Yesterday morning when I went to wark I found Paul Ritson lying full length across his father's grave. His clothes were soaking with dew, and his face was as white as a Feb'uary mist, and stiff and set like, and his hair was frosted over same as a pane in the church window.'

'Never !'

'He was like to take no note of me, but I gave him a shake, and called out, "What, Mr. Paul! why, what, man! what's this!"'

'And whatever did he say ?'

' Say ! Nowt. He get hissel' up—and gay stiff in the limbs he looked, to be sure —and walked off without a word.'

Gubblum, on the tool chest, had removed his pipe from between his lips during the mason's narrative, and listened with a face of blank amazement. ' Weel, that *is* a stiffener,' he said, drawing a long breath.

' What's a stiffener ?' said Job sharply.

' That 'at you're telling for gospel truth.' Then, turning to the blacksmith, the pedlar pointed the shank of his pipe at the mason, and said, ' What morning was it as he found Paul Ritson taking a bath to hissel' in the kirkyard ?'

' Why, yesterday morning,' said the smith.

' Well, he bangs them all at lying,' said Gubblum.

' What dusta say ?' shouted Job with sudden fury.

'As you've telt us a lie,' answered Gubblum.

'Sista, Gubblum, if you don't take that word back I'll—I'll throw you into the watterbutt.'

'And what would I do while you were thrang at that laal job?' asked the pedlar.

The blacksmith interposed. 'Sec a rumpus!' he said; 'you're too sudden in your temper, Job.'

'Some folks are ower much like their namesakes in the Bible,' said Gubblum, resuming his pipe.

'Then what for did he say it warn't true as I found young Ritson yesterday morning wet to the skin in the churchyard?' said Job, ignoring the pedlar.

'Because he warn't there,' said Gubblum.

Job lost all patience. 'Look here,' he said, 'if you're not hankering for a cold

bath on a frosty morning, laal man, I don't
know as you've got any call to say that
again.'

'He warn't there,' the 'laal man'
muttered doggedly.

The blacksmith had plunged his last heat
into the water trough to cool, and a cloud of
vapour filled the smithy. 'Lord A'mighty,'
he said, laughing, 'that's the way some
folks go off—all of a hiss and a smoke.'

'He warn't there,' mumbled the pedlar
again, impervious to the homely similitude.

'How are *you* so certain sure ?' said
Dick of the Syke. 'You warn't there
yourself, I reckon.'

'No ; but I was somewhere else, and so
was Paul Ritson. I slept at the Pack
Horse in Kezzick night afore last, and he
did the same.'

'Did you see him there ?' said the blacksmith.

'No ; but Giles Raisley saw him, and he

warn't astir when Giles went on his morning shift at eight o'clock.'

The blacksmith broke into a loud guffaw. 'Tell us how he was at the Hawk and Heron in London at midsummer.'

'And so he was,' said Gubblum, unabashed.

'Willy nilly, ey ?' said the blacksmith, pausing over the anvil with uplifted hammer, the lurid reflection of the hot iron on his face.

'Maybe he had his reasons for denying hisself,' said Gubblum.

The blacksmith laughed again, tapped the iron with the hand hammer, down came the sledge, and the flakes flew.

Two miners entered the smithy.

'Good morning, John ; are ye gaily ?' said one of them.

'Gaily, gaily ! Why, it's Giles hisself.'

'Giles,' said the pedlar, 'where was Paul Ritson night afore last ?'

'Abed, I reckon,' chuckled one of the newcomers.

'Where abed ?'

'Nay, don't ax me.   Wait—night afore last ? That was the night he slept at Jannet's, wasn't it ?'

Gubblum's eyes twinkled with triumph. 'What did I tell you ?'

'What call had he to sleep at Keswick ?' said the blacksmith ; 'it's no'but four miles from his own bed at the Ghyll.'

'Nay, now, when ye ax the like o' that ——'

Tom, the postman, stopped his grindstone, and snuckered huskily : 'Maybe he's had a fratch with yon brother—yon Hugh.'

'I'm on the morning shift this week, and Mother Jannet she said, "Giles," she said, "the brother of your young master came late last night for a bed."'

'Job, what do you say to that ?' shouted the blacksmith above the pulsating of the bellows, and with the sharp white lights of the leaping flames on his laughing face.

'Say! That they're a pack of liars,' said the mason, catching up his untempered chisels and flinging out of the smithy.

When he had gone, Gubblum removed his pipe and said calmly, 'He's ower much like his Bible namesake in temper—that's the on'y fault of Job.'

The parson, in the field outside, had stood in the turn-rows, resting on his plough handles. He had been drawling 'Bonny lass, canny lass;' but, catching the sound of angry words, he had paused and listened. When Job, the mason, flung away, he returned to his ploughing, and disappeared down the furrow, the boy whistling at his horse's head.

'Why, Mattha, is it thee?' said the blacksmith, observing for the first time the second of the newcomers; 'and how fend ye?'

'Middling weel, John, middling weel,' said Mattha, in a low voice, resting on the edge of the trough.

It was Laird Fisher, more bent than of old, with deeper lines in his grave face and with yet more listless eyes. He had brought two picks for sharpening.

'Got your smelting-house at wark down at the pit, Mattha?' asked the blacksmith.

'Ey, John, it's at wark, it's at wark.'

The miller had turned to go, but he faced about with ready anger.

'Lord, yes, and a pretty pickle you and your gaffer's like to make of me. Wad ye credit it, John? they've built their smelting-house within half a rod of my mill. Half a rod; not a yard mair. When your red hot rubbish is shot down your bank where's it going to go, ey? That's what I want to know—where's it going to go?'

'Why, into your mill, of course,' said

Gubblum, with a wink, from the tool-chest. 'That'll maybe help you to go by fire when you can't raise the wind.'

'Varra good for thee, Gubblum,' laughed the blacksmith.

'I'll have the law on them safe enough,' said the miller.

'And where's your damages to come from ?'

'From the same spot as all the rest of the brass—that's good enough for me.'

Matthew's low voice followed the insinuating guffaw.

'I spoke to Master Hugh yesterday. I telt him all you said about a wall.'

'Well ?'

'He won't build it.'

'Of course not. Why didsta not speak to Paul ?'

'No use in that,' said Matthew faintly.

. 'Nay, young Hugh is gaffer,' exclaimed the blacksmith.

'And Paul has no say in it except finding the brass, ey ?'

'I mak no doubt as you're reet, Dick,' said Matthew meekly.

'It's been just so since the day auld Allan died,' said the blacksmith. 'He hadn't been a week in his grave before Hugh bought up Mattha's royalty in the Hammer Hole, and began to sink for copper. He's never found much ore as I've heard tell on, but he goes ahead laying down his pumping engines, and putting up his cranes, and boring his mill-races, just as if he was proper-ietor of a royal mine.'

'Hugh is the chain-horse, and Paul's no'but the mare in the shafts,' said Gubblum.

'And the money comes somehow,' said Tom o' Dint, who had finished the knife and was testing its edge in whittling a stick.

Matthew got up from his seat.

'I'll come again for the picks, John,' he said quietly, and the old man stepped out of the bright glow into the chill haze.

'Mattha has never been the same since Jaal Mercy left him,' said the blacksmith.

'Any news of her?' asked the pedlar.

'Ax Tom o' Dint; he's the postman, and like to know if anybody in Newlands gets the scribe of a line from the wench,' said the miller.

'Tom shakes his head. You could tell summat, an' you would, ey, Tom?' said the blacksmith, showing his teeth.

'Don't you misliken me,' said the rural messenger in his husky tones; 'I'm none of your peeping Toms.'. And the postman drew up his head with as much pride of office as could be assumed by a gentleman of bowed legs and curtailed stature.

'It baffles me as Mattha hisself could

make nowt of his royalty in the Hammer Hole, if there was owt to make out of it,' said the miller from the gate, buttoning his coat up to his ears.

'I've heard as he had a mind to try his luck again,' said Giles Raisley.

'Nay, nay, nowt of the sort,' said the blacksmith. 'When the laal lass cut away and left the auld chap he lost heart and couldn't bear the sight of the spot where she used to bide. So he started back to his bit place on Coledale Moss. But Hugh Ritson followed him and bought up his royalty—for nowt as they say—and set him to wark for wage in his own sinking —the same that ruined the auld man lang ago.'

'And he's like to see a fortun' come out of it yet,' said Giles.

'It won't be Mattha's fortun', then.'

'Nay, never fear,' said the miner.

Gubblum shook the ashes out of his

pipe, and said meditatively, 'Mattha's like me and the cuckoo.'

'Why, man, how's that?' said the blacksmith, girding his leather apron in a band about his waist. A fresh heat was in the fire; the bellows were belching; the palpitating flames were licking the smoky hood. A twinkle lurked in the blacksmith's eye. 'How's that?' he repeated.

'He's allus stopping short too soon,' said Gubblum. 'My missis, she said to me last back end, "Gubblum," she said, "dusta mind as it's allus summer when the cuckoo is in the garden?" "That's what it is," I said. "Well," she said, "dusta not think it wad allus be summer if the cuckoo could allus be kept here?" "Maybe so," I says; "but easier said nor done." "Shaf on you for a clothead," says she; "nowt so simple. When you get the cuckoo into the garden, build a wall round and keep it in." And that's what I did; and I built

it middling high, too, but it warn't high
enough, for, wad ye think it, one day I
saw the cuckoo setting off, and it just
skimmed the top of that wall by a bare
inch.　Now, if I'd no'but put another
stone——'

A loud peal of laughter was Gubblum's
swift abridgment.　The pedlar tapped the
mouth of his pipe on his thumb-nail, and
smiled under his shaggy brows.

CHAPTER II.

When Parson Christian finished his ploughing the day was far spent. He gave the
boy a shilling as day's wage for leading the
horses, drove the team back to their owner,
Robert Atkinson, paid five shillings for the
day's hire of them, and set out for home.
On the way thither he called at Henry
Walmsley's, the grocery store in the village, and bought half a pound of tea, a can
of coffee, and a stone of sugar; then at
Randal Alston's, the shoemaker's, and paid
for the repairing of a pair of boots and put
them under his arm; finally, he looked in
at the Flying Horse and called for a pot of
ale, and drank it, and smoked a pipe and

had a crack with Tommy Lowthwaite, the publican.

The mist had risen as the day wore on, and now that the twilight was creeping down the valley, the lane to the Vicarage could be plainly seen in its yellow carpeting of fallen leaves. An outer door of the house stood open, and a rosy glow streamed from the fire into the porch. Not less bright was the face within that was waiting to welcome the old vicar home.

' Back again, Greta, back again !' shouted the parson, rolling into the cosy room with his ballast under either arm. ' There— wait—fair play, girl—ah, you rogue !— now that's what I call a *mean* advant- age.'

There was a smack of lips, a little laugh in a silvery voice with a merry lilt in it, and then a deep-toned mutter of affected protestation breaking down into silence and a broad smile.

At arm's length Greta glanced at the parson's burdens, and summoned an austere look.

' Now, didn't I tell you never to do it again ?' she said, with uplifted finger and an air of stern reproof.

' *Did* you now ?' said the parson, with an expression of bland innocence—adding, in an accent of wonderment, ' What a memory I have, to be sure !'

' Leave such domestic duties to your domestic superiors, sir,' said the girl, keeping a countenance of amazing severity. ' Do you hear me, you dear old darling ?'

' I hear, I hear,' said the old man, throwing his purchases on the floor one by one. ' Why, bless me, and here's Mr. Bonnithorne,' he added, lifting his eyes to the chimney-corner, where the lawyer sat toasting his toes. ' Welcome, welcome.'

' Peter, Peter !' called Greta, opening an inner door.

A gaunt old fellow, with only one arm, shambled into the room.

'Peter, take away these things to the kitchen,' said Greta.

The old man glanced down at the parson's purchases with a look of undisguised contempt.

'He's been at it again, mistress,' he said.

The parson had thrown off his coat, and was pushing away his long boots with the boot-jack.

'And how's Mr. Bonnithorne this rusty weather? Wait, Peter, give me the slippers out of the big parcel. I got Randal Alston to cut down my old boots into clock sides, and make me slippers out of the feet. Only sixpence, and see what a cosy pair. Thank you, Peter. So you're well, Mr. Bonnithorne. Odd, you say? Well, it *is*, considering the world of folk who are badly these murky days.'

Peter lifted the boots and fixed them dexterously under the stump of his abridged member. The tea and coffee he deposited in his pockets, and the sugar he carried in his hand.

'There'll be never no living with him,' he muttered in Greta's ear as he passed out. 'Don't know as I mind his going to plough —that's a job for a man with two hands —but the like o' this isn't no master's wark.'

'Dear me!' exclaimed the parson, who was examining his easy-chair preparatory to sitting in it, 'a new cushion—and a bag on the wall for my specs—and a shelf for my pipes—and a—a—what do you call this?'

'An antimacassar, Mr. Christian,' the lawyer answered, smiling, and with uncovered teeth.

'I wondered was he *ever* going to see any difference,' said Greta, with dancing eyes.

'Dear me, and red curtains on the windows, and a clean print counterpane on the settle——'

'A chintz, a chintz,' interposed Greta, with a mock whimper.

'And the old rosewood clock in the corner as bright as a looking-glass, and the big oak cabinet all shiny with oil——'

'Varnish, sir, varnish.'

'And all the carvings on it as fresh as a new pin—St. Peter with his great key, and the rich man with his money-bag trying to defy the fiery furnace.'

'Didn't I say you would scarcely know your own house when you came home again?' said Greta.

She was busying herself at spreading the cloth on the round table and laying the parson's supper.

Parson Christian was revolving on his slippered toes, his eyes full of childlike amazement, and a maturer twinkle of knowingness lurking in that corner of his aged orbs that was not directly under the fire of the girl's sharp, delighted gaze.

'Deary me, have *you* a young lady at home, Mr. Bonnithorne?'

'You know I am a bachelor, Mr. Christian,' said the lawyer demurely.

'So am I, so am I. I never knew any better—not until our old friend Mrs. Lowther died, and left me to take charge of her daughter.'

'Mother should have asked *me* to take charge of Mr. Christian, shouldn't she, Mr. Bonnithorne?' said Greta, with roguish eyes.

'Well, there's something in that,' said the parson with a laugh. ' Peter was getting old and a bit rusty in the hinges, you know, and we were likely to turn out a pair of old crows fit for nothing but to scare good Christians from the district. But Greta came to the musty old house, with

its dust and its cobwebs, and its two old
human spiders, like a slant of sunlight on a
muggy day.   Here's supper—draw up your
chair, Mr. Bonnithorne, and welcome.   It's
my favourite dish—she knows it—barley
broth and a sheep's head, with boiled potatoes and mashed turnips —draw up your
chair—but where's the pot of ale, Greta ?'

' Peter, Peter.'

The other spider presently appeared,
carrying a quart jug with a little mountain of froth—a crater bubbling over and
down the sides.

' Been delving for potatoes to-day, Peter?'
said the parson.

Peter answered with a grumpy nod of his
big head.

' How many bushels ?'

' Maybe a matter of twelve,' muttered
Peter, shambling out.

Then the parson and his guest fell to.

' You're a happy man, Mr. Christian,'

said the lawyer, as Greta left the room on some domestic errand.

Parson Christian shook his head. 'No call for grace,' he said, ' with all the luxuries of life thrown into one's lap—that's the worst of living such a happy life. No trials, no cross—nothing to say but " Soul, take thine ease "—and that's bad when you think of it. . . . Have some sheep's head, Mr. Bonnithorne ; you've not got any tongue— here's a nice sweet bit.'

' Thank you, Mr. Christian. I came round to pay the ten shillings for Joseph Parkinson's funeral sermon last Sunday sennight, and the one pound two half-yearly allowance from the James Bolton charity for poor clergymen.'

' Well, well, they may well say it never rains but it pours,' said the parson. ' I called at Henry Walmsley's and Robert Atkinson's on my way home from the cross roads, and they both paid me their Martin-

14—2

mas quarterage—Henry five shillings, and
Robert seven shillings—and when I dropped
in on Randal Alston to pay for the welting
and soling of my shoes, he said they would
come to one and sixpence, but that he owed
me one and seven pence for veal that Peter
sold him, so he paid me a penny, and we are
clear from the beginning of the world to this
day.'

'I also wanted to speak about our young
friend Greta,' said the lawyer softly. 'I
suppose you are reconciled to losing her?'

'Losing her?—Greta!' said the parson,
laying down his knife. Then smiling, 'Oh,
you mean when Paul takes her—of course,
of course—only the marriage will not be
yet awhile—he said so himself.'

'Marriage with Paul—no,' said Mr. Bonnithorne, clearing his throat and looking grave.

Parson Christian glanced into the lawyer's
face uneasily and lapsed into silence.

'Mr. Christian, you were left guardian

of Greta Lowther by our dear friend her
mother. It becomes your duty to see that
she does the best for her future welfare and
happiness.'

'Surely, surely!' said the parson.

'You are an old man, Mr. Christian, and
she is a young girl. When you and I are
gone, Greta Lowther will still have the
battle of life before her.'

'Please God, please God,' said the parson
faintly.

'Isn't it well that you should see that
she shall have a husband that can fight it
with her side by side?'

'So she shall, so she shall—Paul is a
manly fellow, and as fond of her as of his
own soul—nay, as I tell him, it's idolatry
and a sin before God, his love of the girl.'

'You're wrong, Mr. Christian. Paul
Ritson is no fit husband for Greta. He is
a ruined man. Since his father's death he
has allowed the Ghyll to go to wreck. It

is mortgaged to the last blade of grass. I
know it. Odd, isn't it ?'

Again the smile and the uncovered teeth.

Parson Christian shifted his chair from
the table and gazed into the fire with bewildered eyes. ' I knew he was in trouble,'
he said, ' but I didn't guess that things
wore so grave a look.'

' Don't you see that he is shattered in
mind as well as purse ?' said the lawyer.

' No, no ; I can't say that I do see that.
He's a little absent sometimes, but that's
all. When I talk of Matthew Henry and
discuss his commentaries, or recite the
story of dear Adam Clarke, he is a little—
just a little forgetful—that's all—yes, that
is all.'

' Compared with his brother—what a
difference !' said Mr. Bonnithorne.

' Well, there *is* a difference,' said the
parson.

' Such spirit, such intelligence—he'll be

the richest man in Cumberland one of these days. He has bought up a royalty that is sweating ore, and now he is laying down pumping-engines and putting up smelting-houses, and he is getting standing orders to fix a line of railway for the copper he is fetching up. Odd, isn't it?'

'And where did the money come from?' asked the parson; 'the money to begin?'

The lawyer glanced up sharply. 'It was his share of his father's personalty.'

'A big tree from such a little acorn,' said the parson meditatively, 'and quick growth, too.'

'There's no saying what intelligence and enterprise will not do in *this* world, Mr. Christian,' said the lawyer, who seemed less certain of the next. 'Hugh Ritson is a man of spirit and brains. Now, that's the husband for Greta—that is, if you can get him—and I don't know that you can—but if it were only possible——'

Parson Christian faced about. 'Mr. Bonnithorne,' he said gravely, 'the girl is not up
for sale, and the richest man in Cumberland
can't buy her. The thirty pieces of silver for
which Judas sold his Master may have been
smelted and coined afresh, but not a piece
of that money shall touch fingers of mine.'

'You mistake me, Mr. Christian, believe
me you do,' protested the lawyer, with an
aggrieved expression. 'I was speaking in
our young friend's interests. Whatever
occurs, I beg of you, as a friend and well-
wisher of the daughter of dear Robert
Lowther, now in his grave, never to allow
her to marry Paul Ritson.'

'That shall be as God wills it,' said the
parson quietly.

The lawyer had risen and drawn on his
great-coat.

'She can stay here with me,' continued
the parson.

'No, she should marry now,' said Mr.

Bonnithorne, stepping to the door. 'She is all but of age. It is hardly fair to keep her.'

'Why, what do you mean?' asked the parson, a puzzled look on his face.

'She is rich and she is young. Her wealth can buy comforts, and her youth win pleasures.'

The good old Christian opened wide his great gray eyes with a blank expression. He glanced vacantly about the simple room, rose to his feet, and sat down again.

'I never thought of that before,' he said faintly, and stared long into the fire.

There was a heavy foot on the path outside. The latch was lifted, and Paul Ritson stepped into the room. At the sound of his step Greta tripped through the inner door, all joy and eagerness, to welcome him. The parson got up and held out both hands, the clouds gone from his beaming face.

'Well, good-night,' said the lawyer, opening the door. 'I've four long miles before me. And how dark! how very dark! Odd, isn't it?'

Paul Ritson was in truth a changed man. His face was pale and haggard, and his eyes were bleared and heavy. He dropped with a listless weariness into the chair that Greta drew up to the fire. When he smiled, the lips lagged back to a gloomy repose; and when he laughed, the note of merriment rang hollow and fell short.

'Just in time for a game with me, my lad,' said the parson. 'Greta, fetch the chessboard and box.'

The board was brought, the pieces fixed; the parson settled himself at his ease with slippers on the hearthrug and a handkerchief across his knee.

'Do you know, Paul, I heard a great parl about you to-day?'

'About me! Where?' asked Paul, without much curiosity in his tone.

'At Mr. Proudfoot's smithy, while I was turning the fallows in the meadow, down at the cross roads. Little Mr. Oglethorpe was saying that you slept at the Pack Horse, in Keswick, the night before last; but Mr. Job Sheepshanks, the letter-cutter, said nay, and they had high words indeed, wherein Job called Mr. Oglethorpe all but his proper name, and flung away in high dudgeon.'

Paul moved his pawn and said, ' I never slept at the Pack Horse in my life, Mr. Christian.'

Greta sat knitting at one side of the ingle. The kitten, with a bell attached to a ribbon about its neck, sported with the bows of her dainty slippers. Only the click of the needles, and the tinkle of the bell, and the hollow tick of the great clock in the corner broke the silence.

At last Parson Christian drew himself
up in his chair.

'Well, Paul, man, Paul—deary me,
what a sad move! You're going back,
back, back; once you could beat me five
games to four. Now I can run away with
you.'

The game soon finished, amid a chuckle
from the parson, a bantering word from
Greta, and a loud forced laugh from Paul.

Parson Christian lifted from a shelf a
ponderous tome, bound in leather and en-
cased in green cloth.

'I must make my day's entry,' he said,
'and get off to bed. I was astir before
daybreak this morning.'

Greta crept up behind the old man, and
looked over his shoulder as he wrote:

'Nov. 21.—Retired to my lodging-room
last night, and commended my all to God,
and lay down, and fell asleep; but Peter
minded the heifer that was near to calving;

so he came and wakened me, and we went down and sealed her, and foddered her, and milked her. Spent all day ploughing the low meadow, Peter delving potatoes. Called at the Flying Horse, and sat while I drank one pot of ale and no more, and paid for it. Received ten shillings from Lawyer Bonnithorne for funeral sermon, and one pound two for Bolton charity; also five shillings quarterage from Henry Walmsley, and seven from Robert Atkinson, and a penny to square accounts from Randal Alston, and so retired to my closet at peace with all the world. Blessed be God.'

The parson returned to its shelf the ponderous diary 'made to view his life and actions in,' and called through the inner door for his bedroom candle. A morose voice answered 'Coming,' and presently came.

'Thank you, Peter; and how's the

meeting-house, and who preaches there next Sunday, Peter ?'

Peter grumbled out :

'I don't know as it's not yourself. I passed them my word as you'd exhort 'em a' Sunday afternoon.'

'But nobody has ever asked me. You should have mentioned the matter to me first, Peter, before promising. But never mind, I'm willing, though it's a poor discourse they can get from me.'

Turning to Paul, who sat silent before the fire :

'Peter has left us and turned Methodist,' said the parson; 'he is now Brother Peter Ward, and wants me to preach at the meeting-house. Well, I won't say nay. Many a good ordained clergyman has been dissenting minister as well. Good-night to you. . . . Peter, I wish you to get some whipcord and tie up the reel of my fishing-rod—there it is, on the rafters of the ceiling; and a bit more cord to go round the handle of my whip—it leans against the leads of the neuk window; and, Peter, I'm to go to the mill with the oats to-morrow, and Robin Atkinson has loaned me his shandry and mare. Robin always puts a bushel of grain into the box, but it's light and only small feeding. I wish you to get a bushel of better to mix with it, and make it more worth the mare's labour to eat it. Good-night all; good-night.'

Peter grumbled something beneath his breath and shambled out.

'God bless him!' said Greta presently; and Paul, without lifting his eyes from the fire, said quietly:

'"The lore of Christ and His apostles twelve
He taught : but first he followed it himselve."'

Then there was silence in the little Vicarage. Paul sat without animation until Greta set herself to bewitch him out of his moodiness. Her bright eyes, dancing in the rosy firelight that flickered in the room; her high spirits, bubbling over with delicious teasing and joyous sprightliness; her tenderness, her rippling laughter, her wit, her badinage—all were brought to the defeat and banishment of Paul's heaviness of soul. It was to no purpose. The gloom of the grave face would not be conquered. Paul smiled slightly into the gleaming eyes, and laughed faintly at the pouting lips, and stroked tenderly the soft hair that was glorified into gold in the glint of the firelight; but the old sad look came back once and again.

Greta gave it up at last. She rose from the hassock at his feet.

'Sweetheart,' she said, 'I will go to bed. You are not well to-night, or you are angry, or out of humour.'

She waited a moment, but he did not

speak. Then she made a feeble feint of leaving the room.

At last Paul said :

' Greta, I have something to say.'

She was back at her hassock in an instant. The laughter had gone from her eyes, and left a dewy wistfulness.

' You are unhappy. You have been un-happy a long, long time, and have never told me the cause. Tell me now.'

The heavy face relaxed.

' Whatever put that in your head, little one ?' he asked, in a playful tone, patting the golden hair.

' Tell me now,' she said more eagerly. ' Think of me as a woman fit to share your sorrows, not as a child to be pampered and played with, and never to be burdened with a man's sterner cares. If I am not fit to know your troubles, I am not fit to be your wife. Tell me, Paul, what it is that has taken the sunshine out of your life.'

'The sunshine has not been taken out of my life yet, little woman—here it is,' said Paul lightly, and he drew his fingers through the glistening hair.

The girl's lucent eyes fell.

'You are playing with me,' she said gravely; 'you are always playing with me. Am I so much a child? Are you angry with me?'

'Angry with you, little one? Hardly that, I think,' said Paul, and his voice sank.

'Then tell me, sweetheart. You have something to say—what is it?'

'I have come to ask——'

'Yes?'

He hesitated. His heart was too full to speak. He began again:

'Do you think it would be too great a sacrifice to give up——'

'What?' she gasped.

'Do you remember all you told me about

my brother Hugh—that he said he loved
you ?'

' Well ?' said Greta, with a puzzled
glance.

' I think he spoke truly,' said Paul, and
his voice trembled.

She drew back with agony in every line
of her face.

' Would it be . . . do you think . . .
supposing I went away, far away, and we
were not to meet for a time, a long time
—*never* to meet again—could you bring
yourself to love him and marry him ?'

Greta rose to her feet in agitation.

' Him—love him!—you ask me that—
you !'

The girl's voice broke down into sobs
that seemed to shake her to the heart's
core.

' Greta, darling, forgive me ; I was
blind—I am ashamed.'

' Oh, I could cry my eyes out !' she said,

15—2

wiping away her tears. 'Say you were only playing with me, then; say you were only playing; do say so, do!'

'I will say anything—anything but the same words again—and they nearly killed me to say them.'

'And was this what you came to say?' Greta inquired.

'No, no,' he said, lifted out of his gloom by the excitement; 'but another thing, and it is easier now—ten times easier now —to say it. Greta, do you think if I were to leave Cumberland and settle in another country—Australia or Canada, or somewhere far enough away—that you could give up home, and kindred, and friends, and old associations, and all the dear past, and face a new life in a new world with me? Could you do it?'

Her eyes sparkled. He opened his arms, and she flew to his embrace.

'Is this your answer, little one?' he

said with choking delight. And a pair of
streaming eyes looked up for a brief instant
into his face. ' Then we'll say no more
now. I'm to go to London to-morrow night,
and shall be away four days. When I return
we'll talk again, and tell the good soul who
lies in yonder. Peace be with him, and
sweet sleep, the dear old friend.'

Paul lifted up his hat and opened the
door. His gloom was gone ; his eyes
were alive with animation. The worn
cheeks were aflame. He stood erect, and
walked with the step of a strong man.
Greta followed him into the porch. The
rosy firelight followed her. It flickered
over her golden hair, and bathed her beauty
in a ruddy glow.

' Oh, how free the air will breathe over
there,' he said, ' when all this slavery is
left behind for ever ! You don't understand,
little woman, but some day you shall.
What matter if it is a land of rain and

snow, and tempest? It will be a land of freedom—freedom, and life, and love. And now, Master Hugh, we shall soon be quits—very soon!'

His excitement carried him away, and Greta was too greedy of his joy to check it with questions.

They stood together at the door. The night was still and dark; the trees were noiseless, their prattling leaves were gone. Silent and empty as a vacant street was the unseen road.

Paul held forth his hand to feel if it rained. A withered leaf floated down from the eaves into his palm.

Then a footstep echoed on the path. It went on towards the village. Presently the postman came trudging along from the other direction.

' Good-night, Tom o' Dint,' cried Paul cheerily.

Tom stopped and hesitated.

' Who was it I hailed on the road ?' he asked.

' When ?'

' Just now.'

' Nay, who was it ?'

' I thought it was yourself.'

The little man trundled on in the dark.

' My brother, no doubt,' said Paul, and pulled the door after him.

CHAPTER III.

NEXT morning a bright sun shone on the frosty landscape. The sky was blue and the air was clear.

Hugh Ritson sat in his room at the back of the Ghyll, with its window looking out on the fell side and on the river under the leafless trees beneath. The apartment had hardly the appearance of a room in a Cumbrian homestead. It was all but luxurious in its appointments. The character of its contents gave it something of the odour of a bygone age. Besides books on many shelves, prints, pictures in water and oil, and mirrors of various shapes, there were tapestry on the inside of the door, a bust of Dante above a cabinet of black oak, a piece of bas-relief in soapstone, a gargoyle in wood, a brass censer, a mediæval lamp with open mouth, and a small ivory crucifix nailed to the wall above the fire.

Hugh himself sat at an organ, his fingers wandering aimlessly over the keys, his eyes gazing vacantly out at the window.

'May I intrude?' said the meek voice of Mr. Bonnithorne from without.

'Come in,' said the player. The lawyer entered and walked to a table in the middle of the floor. Hugh Ritson finished the movement he was playing, and then rose from the organ and drew an easy chair to the fire.

'Brought the deed?' he asked quietly, Mr. Bonnithorne still standing.

'I have, my dear friend, and something yet more important.'

Hugh glanced up : through his constant
smile Mr. Bonnithorne was obviously agitated. Dropping his voice, the lawyer
added, ' Copies of the three certificates.'

Hugh smiled faintly. ' Good ; we will
discuss the certificates first,' he said, and
drew his dressing-gown leisurely about
him.

Mr. Bonnithorne began to unfold some
documents. He paused ; his eye was
keen and bright ; he seemed to survey
his dear friend with some perplexity ; his
glance was shadowed by a certain look of
distrust ; but his words were cordial and
submissive, and his voice was, as usual, low
and meek. ' What a wonderful man you
are. And how changed ! It is only a few
months since I had to whip up your lagging
spirits at a great crisis. And now you leave
me far behind. Not the least anxious !
How different I am, to be sure. It was
this very morning my correspondent sent

me the copies, and yet I am here, five miles from home. And when the post arrived I declare to you that such was my eagerness to know if our surmises were right that——'

Hugh interrupted in a quick cold voice : 'That you were too nervous to open his letter, and fumbled it back and front for an hour—precisely.'

Saying this, Hugh lifted his eyes quickly enough to encounter Mr. Bonnithorne's glance, and when they fell again an expression of quiet scorn was playing about his mouth.

'Give me the papers,' said Hugh, and he stretched forward his hand without shifting in his seat.

'Well, really, you are—really——'

Hugh raised his eyes again. Mr. Bonnithorne paused, handed the documents, and shuffled uneasily into a seat.

One by one Hugh glanced hastily over

three slips of paper. 'This is well,' he said quietly.

'Well? I should say so indeed. What could be better? I confess to you that until to-day I had some doubts. Now I have none.'

'Doubts? So you had doubts,' said Hugh drily. 'They disturbed your sleep, perhaps?'

The lurking distrust in Mr. Bonnithorne's eyes openly displayed itself, and he gazed full into the face of Hugh Ritson with a searching look that made little parley with his smile. 'Then one may take a man's inheritance without qualm or conviction? Odd, isn't it?'

Hugh pretended not to hear, and began to read aloud the certificates in his hand. 'Let me see, this is first—Registration of Birth.'

Mr. Bonnithorne interrupted. 'Luckily, very luckily, the registration of birth *is* first.'

Hugh read—

'Name, Paul. Date of birth, August 14, 1845. Place of birth, Russell Square, London. Father's name, Robert Lowther. Mother's name, Grace Lowther; maiden name, Ormerod.

'Then this comes second—Registration of Marriage.'

Mr. Bonnithorne rose in his eagerness and rubbed his hands together at the fire. 'Yes, *second*,' he said, with evident relish.

Hugh read calmly:

'Allan Ritson—Grace Ormerod—Registrar's office, Bow Street, Strand, London—June 12th, 1847.'

'What do you say to that?' asked Mr. Bonnithorne, in an eager whisper.

Hugh continued without comment. 'And this comes last—Registration of Birth.'

'Name, Hugh—March 25th, 1848—Holme, Ravenglass, Cumberland—Allan Ritson—Grace Ritson (Ormerod).'

'There you have the case in a nutshell,' said Mr. Bonnithorne, dropping his voice. 'Paul is your half-brother, and the son of Lowther. You are Allan Ritson's heir, born within a year of your father's marriage. Can anything be clearer?'

Hugh remained silently intent on the documents. 'Were these copies made at Somerset House?' he asked.

Mr. Bonnithorne nodded.

'And your correspondent can be relied upon?'

'Assuredly. A solicitor in excellent practice.'

'Was he told what items he had to find, or did he make a general search?'

'He was told to find the marriage or marriages of Grace Ormerod, and to trace her offspring.'

'And these were the only entries.'

Mr. Bonnithorne nodded again.

Hugh twirled the papers in his fingers,

and then placed two of them side by side. His face wore a look of perplexity. ' I am puzzled,' he said.

' What puzzles you ?' said Mr. Bonnithorne. ' Can anything be plainer ?'

' Yes. By these certificates I am two and a half years younger than Paul. I was always taught that there was only a year between us.'

Mr. Bonnithorne smiled, and said in a superior tone :

' An obvious ruse, my dear young friend.'

The dear young friend laughed slightly.

' You think a child is easily deceived— true !'

Mr. Bonnithorne preserved a smiling face.

' Now, I shall proceed to the payment of the legacy, and you, no doubt, to the institution of your claim.'

' No,' said Hugh Ritson, with emphasis, rising to his feet.

'You know that if a bastard dies seized of an estate, the law justifies his title. He is then the bastard *eigne*. You must eject this man.'

'No,' said Hugh Ritson again.

The lawyer glanced up inquiringly, and Hugh added :

'That shall come later. Meantime the marriage must be brought about.'

'Your own marriage with Greta ?'

'Paul's.'

'Paul's ?' said Mr. Bonnithorne, the very suppression of his tone giving it additional emphasis.

'Paul's,' repeated Hugh with grim composure. 'He shall marry her.'

The lawyer had risen once more, and was now face to face with Hugh Ritson, glancing into his eyes with eager scrutiny.

'You cannot mean it,' he said at length, with a short, soft gurgle.

'And why not ?' said Hugh placidly.

'Because Paul is her brother—at least her half-brother.'

'They don't know that.'

Mr. Bonnithorne's breath seemed to be arrested.

'But we know it, and we can't stand by and witness their marriage,' he said at length.

Hugh Ritson leaned with his back to the fire.

'We can, and shall,' he said, and not a muscle of his face moved.

Mr. Bonnithorne surveyed his friend from head to foot, and then his own countenance relaxed.

'You are trifling; but it will be no trifle to them when they learn that their billing and cooing must end. And from such a cause, too. It will be a terrible shock. The only question is, whether it would not be more humane to say nothing of the impediment until we have brought about

another match.   Last night, at Parson
Christian's, I did what I could for you.'

Hugh smiled in return ; a close observer
might have seen that his was a cold mockery
of the lawyer's own smile.

' Yes, you were always humane, Bonnithorne, and now your sensibilities are
shocked.   But when I spoke of marriage I
meant the ceremony.   Nothing more.'

The lawyer's eyes twinkled.

' I think I understand.   You intend to
separate them at the church door—perhaps
at the altar rail.   It is a shocking revenge.
My very skin creeps.'

Hugh laughed lightly, and walked to the
window.   A slant of sunshine fell on his
up-turned face.   When he turned his head
and broke silence he spoke in a deep, harsh
voice.

' I was humane, too.   When she spoke of
marriage with Paul I hinted at an impediment.   She ridiculed the idea; scoffed at

it.' Another light laugh, and then a stern solemnity. 'She insulted me—palpably, grossly, brutally. What did she say? Didn't I tell you before? Why, she said—ha, ha! would you believe it?—she said she'd rather marry a ploughboy than such a gentleman as me. That was her very word.'

Hugh Ritson's face was now dark with passion, while laughter was on his lips.

'She *shall* marry her ploughboy, to her lifelong horror and disgrace. I promised her as much, and I shall keep my word.'

'A terrible revenge,' muttered the lawyer, twitching uneasily at his finger nails.

'Tut, you don't know to what lengths love may go. Even the poor feeble infant hearts of men whose minds are a blank can carry them any length in the devotion or the revenge of love.' He paused, and then added in a low tone, 'She has outraged my love.'

16—2

'Surely not past forgiveness,' interrupted
the lawyer nervously. The smile had disappeared. 'It would be a life-long injury.
And she is a woman too.'

Hugh faced about.

'But he is a man ; and I have my reckoning with him also.' Hugh Ritson strode
across the room, and then stopped suddenly.
'Look you, Bonnithorne, you said that with
all your confidence on the night of my
father's death, you had your doubts until
to-day. But I had never a moment's doubt.
Why ? Because I had assurance from my
mother's own lips. To me ? No, but
worse; to him. He knows well he is not
my father's heir. He has known it since
the hour of my father's death. He knows
that I know it. Yet he has kept the lands
to this day.' Another uneasy perambu-
lation. 'Do you think of that when you
talk of revenge ? Manliness ? He has
none. He is a pitiful, truculent, grovelling

coward, ready to buy profit at any price.
He has robbed me of my inheritance. He
stands in my place. He is a living lie.
Revenge ? It will be retribution.'

Hugh Ritson's composure was gone. His
voice quivered and his face was discoloured.
Mr. Bonnithorne, not easily cowed, dropped
his eyes before him. ' Terrible, terrible !'
he muttered again, and added with more
assurance, ' But you know, I have always
urged you to assert your right to the inheritance.'

Hugh was striding about the room,
his infirm foot trailing heavily after
him.

' Bonnithorne,' he said, pausing, ' when
a woman has outraged the poor weak heart
of one of the waifs whom fate flings into the
gutter, he sometimes throws a cup of vitriol
into her face, saying, '' If she is not for me
she is not for another :'' or '' Where she
has sinned, there let her suffer.'' *That* is

revenge ; it is the feeble device of a man who thinks in his simple soul that when beauty is gone loathing is at hand.'

Another light trill of laughter.

' But the cup of retribution is not to be measured by the cup of vitriol.'

Mr. Bonnithorne fumbled his papers nervously, and repeated beneath his breath, ' Terrible, terrible !'

' She has wronged me, Bonnithorne, and he has wronged me. They shall marry and they shall separate ; and henceforward they shall walk together and yet apart, a gulf dividing them from each other, yet a wider gulf dividing both from the world ; and so on until the end, and he and I and she and I are quits.'

' Terrible, terrible !' the lawyer mumbled again. ' All nature rises against it.'

' Is it so ? Then be it so,' said Hugh, the flame subsiding from his cheek, and a cold smile creeping afresh about his lips.

'Your sense of justice would have been answered, perhaps, if I had turned this bastard adrift penniless and a beggar, stopped the marriage, and taken by strategy the woman I could not win by love.' The smile faded away. ' That would have been better than the cup of vitriol, but not much better. You are a man of the world.'

' It is a terrible revenge,' the lawyer muttered again—this time with a different intonation. It had been fear and horror before ; now it was a kind of pride in his friend's cleverness.

' I repeat they shall *marry*. No more than that,' said Hugh. ' I would outrage nature as little as I would shock the world.'

The sun had crept round to where the organ stood in one corner of the room. Hugh's passion had gradually subsided. He sidled on to the stool and began to play softly. A knock came to the door, and old Laird Fisher entered.

'The gentleman frae Crewe is down at the pit about t'engine in the smelting mill,' said the old man.

'Say I shall be with him in half an hour,' said Hugh, and Laird Fisher left the room. Then Hugh put the papers in his pocket.

'We have wasted too much time over the certificates—they can wait—where's the deed of mortgage?—I must have the money to pay for the new engine.'

'It is here,' said the lawyer, and he spread a parchment on the table.

Hugh glanced hastily over it, and touched a handbell. When the maid appeared he told her to go to Mr. Paul, who was thatch-ing in the stackyard, and say he wished to see him at once. Then he returned to the organ, and played a tender air. His touch was both light and strenuous.

'Any news of his daughter?' said Mr. Bonnithorne, sinking his voice to a whisper.

'Whose daughter?' said Hugh, pausing, and looking over his shoulder.

'The old man's—Laird Fisher's.'

'Strangely enough—yes. A letter came this morning.'

Hugh Ritson stopped playing, and thrust his hand into an inner pocket. But Mr. Bonnithorne hastened to show that he had no desire to pry into another man's secrets.

'Pray don't trouble. Perhaps you'd rather not—just tell me in a word how things are shaping.'

Hugh laughed a little derisively, unfolded a sheet of scented writing-paper, with ornamented border, and began to read :

'"I am writing to thank you very much——" Here,' tossing the letter to the lawyer, 'read it for yourself.' Then he resumed his playing.

Mr. Bonnithorne fixed his nose-glasses, and read :

' I am writing to thank you very much for your kind remembrance of me, it was almost like having your company, I live in hopes of seeing you soon, when are you coming to me? Sometimes I think you will never, never come, and then I can't help crying though I try not to, and I don't cry much. I don't go out very often London is far away, six miles, there are nice people here and nice children. Only think when my trouble is over and you come and take me home. How is poor father, does he look much older does he fret for me now? I wonder will he know me. I am quite well only there is something the matter in my eyes. Sometimes when I wake up I can't see plain. Don't be long writing. My eyes are very sore and red to-day, and it is oh so lonely in this strange place. Mrs. Drayton is kind to me. Good-bye. She has a son but he is always at meets, that is races, and

I have never seen him. Write soon to your loving Mercy. The time is near.'

Hugh played on while Mr. Bonnithorne read. The lawyer, when he came to the end, handed the letter back with the simple comment :

' Came this morning, you say ? It was written last Tuesday—nearly a week ago.'

Hugh nodded his head over his shoulder, and continued to play. He swayed to and fro with an easy grace to the long sweeps of the music until the door opened sharply and Paul entered with a firm step. Then he rose, picked a pen from the inkstand and dipped it in the ink.

Paul wore a suit of rough light cloth, with leggings, and a fur cap, which he did not remove. His face was pale ; decision sat on every line of it.

' Excuse me, Mr. Bonnithorne, if I don't shake hands,' he said in his deep voice, ' I'm at work, and none too clean.'

'Ah, the horny hand of toil is honourable,' said the lawyer in a tone of suavity.

Paul answered the clap-trap with a look of undisguised contempt, but said nothing.

'This,' said Hugh Ritson, standing between them and twiddling the pen in his fingers, 'this is the deed I spoke of yesterday. You sign there,' pointing to a blank space in front of a little wafer.

Then he placed one hand firmly on the upper part of the parchment, as if to steady it, and held out the pen.

Paul made no approach to accepting it. He stretched forward, took hold of the document and lifted it, casting Hugh's hand aside.

Hugh watched him closely.

'The usual formality,' he said lightly, 'nothing more.'

Paul passed his eye rapidly over the deed. Then he turned to the lawyer.

'Is this the fourth or fifth mortgage that

has been drawn ?' he inquired, still holding
the parchment before him.

'Really, I can't say—I presume it is
the—really, I hardly remember——'

Mr. Bonnithorne's suavity of tone and
customary smile broke down into silence
and a look of lowering anxiety.

Paul glanced steadfastly into his face.

'But *I* remember,' he said with composure more embarrassing than violence.
'It is the fifth. The Holme farm was
first, and then came Goldscope. Hindscarth was mortgaged to the last ear of
corn, and then it was the turn for Coledale.
Now it's the Ghyll itself, I see, house and
buildings.'

Hugh Ritson's face underwent a livid
change, but his tone was unruffled as he
said :

'If you please, we will come to business.'
Then with a sinister smile, 'You resemble
the French counsel — you begin every

speech at the Creation. " Let us go on to the Deluge," said the judge.'

'To the Deluge!' said Paul, and he turned his head slowly to where Hugh stood, holding the pen in one hand and rapping the table with the knuckles of the other. 'Rather unnecessary. We're already under water.'

The passion in Hugh Ritson's face dropped to a look of sullen anger. But he mastered his voice, and said quietly :

'The engineer from Crewe is waiting for me at the pit. I have wasted the whole morning over these formalities. Come, come, let us have done. Mr. Bonnithorne will witness the signature.'

Paul had not shifted his steadfast gaze from his brother's face. Hugh dogged his glance at first, and then met it with an expression of audacity.

Still holding the parchment before him, Paul said quietly :

' To-night I leave home for London, and shall be absent four days. Can this business wait until my return ?'

'No, it can't,' said Hugh with emphasis.

Paul dropped his voice.

' Don't take that tone with me, I warn you.. Can the business wait ?'

' I mean what I say—it can *not*.'

' On my return I may have something to tell you that will affect this and the other deeds. Once more, can it wait ?'

' Will you sign—yes or no ?' said Hugh, his face now dark with anger.

Paul looked steady and straight into his brother's eyes.

' You are draining away my inheritance —you are——'

At this word, Hugh's smouldering temper was afire.

' *Your* inheritance !' he broke out in his bitterest tones. ' It is late in the day to talk of that. *Your* inheritance——'

But he stopped. The expression of audacity gave place to a look of blank bewilderment. Paul had torn the parchment from top to bottom and flung it on the table, and in an instant was walking out of the room.

CHAPTER IV.

Paul Ritson returned to the stackyard, and worked vigorously three hours longer. A stack had been stripped by a recent storm, and he thatched it afresh with the help of a labourer and a boy. Then he stepped indoors, changed his clothes, and filled a travelling bag. When this was done, he went in search of the stableman. Natt was in his stable, whistling as he polished his harness.

'Bring the trap round to the front at seven,' he said, 'and put my bag in at the back ; you'll find it in the hall.'

By this time the night had closed in, and the young moon showed faintly over the head of Hindscarth. The wind was rising.

Paul returned to the house, ate, drank, and smoked. Then he rose and walked upstairs, and knocked at the door of his mother's room.

Mrs. Ritson was alone. A lamp burned on the table, and cast a sharp white light on her face. That face was worn and very pale. Lines were ploughed deep on it. She was kneeling, but she rose as Paul entered. He bent his head and kissed her forehead. There was a book before her; a rosary was in her hand. The room was without fire. It was chill and cheerless, and only sparsely furnished—sheep-skin rugs on the floor, texts on the wall, a carved oak clothes-chest in one corner, two square high-backed chairs and a small table, a bed, and no more.

'I am going off, mother,' said Paul; 'the train leaves in a hour.'

'When do you return?' said Mrs. Ritson.

'Let me see—this is Saturday—I shall be back on Wednesday evening.'

'God be with you,' she said in a fervent voice.

'Mother, I spoke to Greta last night, and she promised. We shall soon be free of this tyranny. Already the first link of the chain is broken. He called me into his room this morning to sign a mortgage on the Ghyll, and I refused.'

'And yet you are about to go away, and leave everything in his hands!'

Mrs. Ritson sat down, and Paul put his hand tenderly on her head.

'Better that than to have it wrested from me inch by inch—to hold the shadow of an inheritance while he grasps the substance. He knows all. His dark hints are not needed to tell me that.'

'Yet he is silent,' said Mrs. Ritson, and her eyes fell on to her book. 'And surely it is for my sake that he is so—if in truth he knows all. Is he not my son? And is not my honour his honour?'

17—2

Paul shook his head.

' If the honour of twenty mothers, as true and dear as you, were the stepping-stones to his interest, over those stones he would go. No, no; it is not honour, whether yours or his, that keeps him silent.'

Mrs. Ritson glanced up.

' Are you not too hard on him ? He is guiltless in the eye of the world, and that at least should plead for him. Forgive him. Do not leave your brother in anger !'

' I have nothing to forgive,' said Paul. ' Even if he knew nothing I should still go away and leave everything. I could not live any longer under the shadow of this secret, bound by an oath. I would go, as I shall go now, with sealed lips, but a free heart. He should have his own before man —and I mine before God.'

Mrs. Ritson sat in silence; her lips

trembled perceptibly, and her eyelids quivered.

'I shall soon leave you, my dear son,' she said in a tremulous voice.

'Nay, nay, you shall not,' he answered in an altered tone, half of raillery, half of tenderness; 'you are coming with us—with Greta and me—and over there the roses will bloom again in your white cheeks.'

Mrs. Ritson shook her head.

'I shall soon leave you, dearest,' she repeated, and told her beads.

He tried to dispel her sadness; he laughed, and she smiled feebly; he patted her head playfully. But she came back to the same words: 'I shall soon leave you.'

The moon was shining at the full when he lifted his hat to go. It was sailing through a sky of fibrous cloud. The wind was high, and rattled the empty boughs of the trees against the window. Keen frost was in the air.

'I shall see my father's old friend in London on Monday, and be back on Wednesday. Good-bye. Keep a good heart. Good-bye.'

She wept on his breast and clung to him.

'Good-bye, good-bye,' he repeated, and tried to disengage himself from her embrace.

But she clung the closer. It was as if she was to see him no more.

'Good-bye,' she sobbed, and with the tears in his own eyes he laughed at her idle fears. 'Ha, ha, ha, one would think I was going for life—ha, ha——'

There was a scream on the frosty air without. His laugh died on his lips.

'What was that?' he said, and drew a sharp breath.

She lifted her face, whiter now than ever, and with tearless eyes.

'It was the cry of the bird that foretells death,' she said in a whisper.

He laughed a little—boisterously.

' Nay, nay ; you will be well and happy yet.' Then he broke away.

Natt was sitting in the trap, and it was drawn up in the courtyard to the door. He was looking through the darkness at some object in the distance, and when Paul came up he was not at first conscious of his master's presence.

' What were you looking at, Natt ?' said Paul, pulling on his gloves.

' I war wond'rin' whether lang Dick o' the Syke had kindled a fire to-night, or whether yon lowe on the side of the Causey were frae the new smelting-house.'

Paul glanced over the horse's head. A deep glow stood out against the fell. All around was darkness.

' The smelting-house, I should say,' said Paul, and jumped to his seat beside Natt.

By one of the lamps that the trap carried he looked at his watch.

' A quarter-past seven. It will be smart driving, but you can give the mare her own time coming back.' Then he took the reins, and in another moment they were gone.

CHAPTER V.

AT eight o'clock that night the sky was brilliantly lit up, and the sound of many voices was borne on the night wind. The red flare came from the Syke; the mill was afire. Showers of sparks and sheets of flame were leaping and streaming into the sky. Men and women were hurrying to and fro, and the women's shrill cries mingled with the men's hoarse shouts. At intervals the brightness of the glare faded, and then a column of choking smoke poured out and was borne away on the wind. Dick, the miller, was there, with the scorching heat reddening his wrathful face. John Proudfoot had raised a ladder against the mill, and, hatchet in hand, was going to cut away the cross-trees; but the heat drove him back. The sharp snap of the flames told of timbers being ripped away.

'No use—it's gone,' said the blacksmith, dragging the ladder behind him.

'I telt them afore what their damned smelting-house would do for me,' said the miller, striding about in his impotent rage.

Parson Christian was standing by the gate on the windward side of the mill-yard, with Laird Fisher beside him, looking on in silence at the leaping flames.

'The wind is from the south,' he said, 'and a spark of the hot refuse shot down the bank has been blown into the mill.'

The mill was a wooden structure, and the fire held it like a serpent in its grip. People were coming and going from the darkness into the red glare, and out of the glare into the darkness. Among them was one stalwart figure that none noticed in the general confusion.

'Have you a tarpaulin ?' said this man, addressing those about him.

'There's a big one on the stack at Cole-dale,' answered another.

'Run for it.'

'It's of no use.'

'Damme, run for it.'

The tone of authority was not to be ignored. In three minutes a huge tarpaulin was being dragged behind a dozen men.

'Lay hold of the ropes and let us dip it into the river,' shouted the same voice above the prevailing clangour. It was done. Dripping wet, the tarpaulin was pulled into the mill-yard.

'Where's your ladder ? Quick !'

The ladder was raised against the scorching wooden walls.

'Be ready to throw me the ropes,' shouted the deep voice.

A firm step was set on the lowest rung. There was a crackle of glass, and then a cloud of smoke streamed out of a broken window. For an instant the bright glare was obscured. But it burst forth afresh, and leapt with great wide tongues into the sky.

'The sheets are caught,' shouted the miller.

They were flying round with the wind. A line of flame seemed to be pursuing them.

'Who is the man on the ladder—dusta know?' cried John Proudfoot.

'I dunnot,' answered the miller.

At that instant Hugh Ritson came up. The smoke was gone, and now a dark figure could be dimly seen high up on the mill side. He seized the crosstrees with both hands, and swung himself on to the raking roof.

'Now for the ropes,' he shouted.

The flame burst out again and illumined the whole sky; the dark mass of the fells could be seen far overhead, and the waters of the river in the bed of the valley glowed like amber. The stalwart figure stood out in the white light against the red glare, holding on to the crosstrees on the top of the mill, and with a wheel of crackling fire careering beside him.

There could be no doubt of his identity, with the light on his strong face and tawny hair.

'It's Paul Ritson.' shouted many a voice.

'Damme, the ropes—quick.'

The ropes were thrown and caught, and thrown again to the other side. Then the dripping tarpaulin was drawn over the mill until it covered the top and half the sides. The wheel burnt out, and the iron axle came to the ground with a plunge.

The fire was conquered; the night sky grew black; the night wind became voiceless. Then the busy throng had time for talk.

' Where's Paul ?' asked Parson Christian.

' Aye, where is he ?' said the miller.

' He's a stunner, for sure—where is he ?' said the blacksmith.

None knew. When the flames began to fade he was missed. He had gone —none knew where.

' Nine o'clock,' said Parson Christian, turning his face towards home. ' Sharp work while it lasted, my lads.'

Then there was the sound of wheels, and Natt drove his trap to the gate of the mill yard.

' You've just missed it, Natt,' said John Proudfoot; ' where have you been ?'

' Driving the master to the train.'

Hugh Ritson was standing by. Everyone glanced from him to Natt.

' The train ?—master ? What do you mean ? Who ?'

' Who ? Why, Master Paul,' said Natt, with a curl of the lip. ' I reckon it could scarce be Master Hugh.'

' When ? What train ?' said Parson Christian.

' The eight o'clock to London.'

' Eight o'clock ? London ?'

' Don't I speak plain ?'

' And has he gone ?'

' I's warrant he's gone.'

Consternation sat on every face but Natt's.

CHAPTER VI.

NEXT day was Sunday, and after morning service a group of men gathered about the church porch to discuss the events of the night before. In the evening the parlour of the Flying Horse was full of dalespeople, and many a sapient theory was then and there put forth to account for the extraordinary coincidence of the presence of Paul Ritson at the fire and his alleged departure by the London train.

Hugh Ritson was not seen abroad that day. But early on Monday morning he hastened to the stable, called on Natt to saddle a horse, sprang on its back, and galloped away towards the town.

The morning was bitterly cold, and the rider was buttoned up to the throat. The air was damp; a dense veil of vapour lay on the valley and hid half the fells; the wintry dawn, with its sunless sky, had not the strength to rend it asunder; the wind had veered to the north, and was now dank and icy. A snowstorm was coming.

The face of Hugh Ritson was wan and jaded. He leaned heavily forward in the saddle; the biting wind was in his eyes; he had a fixed look, and seemed not to see the people whom he passed on the road.

Dick o' the Syke was grubbing among the fallen wreck of the charred and dismantled mill. When Hugh rode past him he lifted his eyes and muttered an oath beneath his breath. Old Laird Fisher was trundling a wheelbarrow on the bank of the smelting-house. The head-gear of the pit-shaft was working. As Hugh passed the smithy, John Proudfoot was standing, hammer in hand, by the side of a wheelless waggon upheld by poles. John was saying, ' Wonder what see place Mister Paul slept a' Saturday night — I reckon that wad settle all ;' and a voice from inside the smithy answered, ' Nowt of the sort, John ; it's a fate I tell tha.' The pedlar's pony was standing by the hasp of the gate.

Never once lifting his eyes, with head bent and compressed lips, Hugh Ritson rode on in the teeth of the coming storm. There was another storm within that was uprooting every emotion of his soul. When he came to the Vicarage he drew up sharply and rapped heavily on the gate. Brother Peter came shambling out at the speed of six steps a minute.

' Mr. Christian at home ?' asked Hugh.

' Don't know as he is,' said Peter.

' Where is he ?'

' Don't know as I've heeard.'

' Tell him I'll call as I come back, in two hours.'

' Don't know as I'll see him.'

' Then go and look for him,' shouted Hugh impatiently, bringing down the whip on the flank of the horse.

Brother Peter Ward turned about sulkily. ' Don't know as I will,' he grumbled, and trudged back into the house.

Then Hugh Ritson rode on. A thin sleet began to fall, and it drove hard into his face. The roads were crisp, and the horse sometimes stumbled; but the rider pressed on.

In less than half an hour he was riding into the town. The people who were standing in groups in the market-place parted and made space for him. They hailed him with respectful salutations: He responded curtly or not at all. Notwithstanding his long ride his face was still pale, and his lips were livid. He stopped at the courtyard leading to the front of the Packhorse. Old Willie Calvert, the innkeeper, stood there, and touched his cap when Hugh approached him.

' My brother Paul slept here a few nights ago, I hear,' said Hugh.

' So he did,' said the innkeeper.

' What night was it ?'

' What night ? Let me see—it were a week come Wednesday.'

' Did you see him yourself ?'

' Nay, I were lang abed.'

' Who did—Mistress Calvert ?'

' Ey, she did for sure—Jannet ' (calling up the court). ' She'll tell ye all the ins and oots.'

A comfortable-looking elderly body in a white cap and print apron came to the door.

' You saw my brother—Paul, you know —when he slept at your house last Wednesday night ?'

' Yes, surely,' said Jannet.

'What did he say?'

'Nay, nowt. It was varra late—maybe twelve o'clock—and I was bolting up and had the cannel in my hand to get me to bed, and a rap came, and when I opened the door who should it be but Mister Paul. He said he wanted a bed, but he seem't to be in the doldrums and noways keen for a crack, so I ax't na questions, but just took him to the little green room over the snug and bid him good-night.'

'And next morning—did you see him then?' said Hugh.

'No'but a minute when he paid his bed, for he had nowther bite nor sup in the house.'

'Did he look changed?—anything different about him?'

'Nay, nowt but in low feckle someways, and maybe summat different dressed.'

'How different? What did he wear that night?' Pale as Hugh Ritson's face had been before, it was now white as a face in moonlight.

'Maybe a pepper-and-salt tweed coat, but I can't rightly call to mind at the minute.'

Hugh's great eyes stared out of his head. His tongue clave to his mouth, and for the moment denied him speech.

'Thank you, Mistress Calvert. Here, Willie, my man, drink my health with the missis.'

So saying, he tossed a silver coin to the innkeeper, wheeled about, and rode off.

'I cannut mak nowther head nor tail o' this,' said the old man.

'Of what—the brass?' said Jannet.

'Nay, but that's soond enough for sure, auld lass.'

'Then just thoo leave other folks's business to theirselves, and come thy ways in with thee. Thoo wert allus thrang a-meddlin'.'

The innkeeper had gone indoors and drawn himself a draught of ale.

'I allus like to see the ins and oots o' things,' he observed with a twinkle in his eye and the pot to his mouth.

'Mind as you're not ower keen at seein' the ins and oots o' that pewter.'

'I'll be keerful, auld lass.'

Hugh Ritson's horse went clattering over the stones of the streets until it came to the house of Lawyer Bonnithorne. Then Hugh drew up sharply, jumped from the saddle, tied the reins to the loop in the gate-pier, and rang the bell. In another minute he was standing in the breakfast-room, which was made comfortable by a glowing fire. Mr. Bonnithorne, in dressing-gown and slippers, rose from his easy-chair with a look of surprise.

'Did you hear of the fire at the mill on Saturday night?' asked Hugh in a faltering voice.

Mr. Bonnithorne nodded his head.

'Very unlucky, very,' said the lawyer. 'The man will want recompensè, and the law will support him.   Odd, isn't it ?'

'Tut—a bagatelle,' said Hugh, with a gesture of impatience.

'Of course, if you say so——'

'You've heard nothing about Paul ?'

Mr. Bonnithorne answered with a shake of his yellow head and a look of inquiry.

Then Hugh told him of the man at the fire, and of Natt's story when he drove up in the trap.   He spoke with visible embarrassment, and in a voice that could scarcely support itself.   But the deep fear that had come over him had not yet taken hold of the lawyer.   Mr. Bonnithorne listened with a bland smile of amused in- . credulity.   Hugh stopped with a shudder.

'What are you thinking ?' he asked nervously.

'That Natt lied.'

'As well say that the people at the fire lied.'

'No ; you yourself saw Paul there.'

'Bonnithorne, like all keen-eyed men, you are short-sighted. I have something more to tell you. The people at the Pack Horse say that Paul slept at their house last Wednesday night. Now I know that he slept at home.'

The lawyer smiled again.

'A mistake as to the night,' he said ; 'What can be plainer ?'

'Don't wriggle, Bonnithorne ; look the facts in the face.'

'Facts ?—a coincidence in evidence—a common error.'

'Would to God it were !' Hugh strode about the room in obvious perturbation, his eyes bent on the ground. 'Bonnithorne, what is the place where the girl Mercy lives ?'

'An inn at Hendon.'

' Do they call it the Hawk and Heron ?'

' They do. The old woman Drayton keeps it.'

Hugh Ritson's step faltered. He listened with a look of stupid consternation.

' Did I never tell you that the pedlar Oglethorpe said he saw Paul at the Hawk and Heron in Hendon ?'

The lawyer dropped back into his seat without a word. Conviction was taking hold of him.

' What do the folks say ?' he asked at length.

' Say ? That it was a ghost, a wraith, twenty things—the idiots !'

' What do *you* say, Mr. Ritson ?'

' That it was *another man.*'

The lawyer remained sitting, his eyes fixed and vacant.

' What then ? What if it *is* another man ? Resemblances are common. We are all brothers. For example, there are numbers of persons like myself in the world. Odd, isn't it?'

'Very,' said Hugh with a hard laugh.

'And what if there exists a man resembling your half-brother Paul so closely that on three several occasions he has been mistaken for him by competent witnesses— what does it come to?'

Hugh paused.

'Come to? God knows. I want to find out. Who is this man? What is he? Where does he come from? What is his business here? Why, of all places on this wide earth, does he, of all men alive, haunt my house like a shadow?'

Hugh Ritson was still visibly perturbed.

'There's more in this matter than either of us knows,' he said.

Mr. Bonnithorne watched him for a moment in silence.

'I think you draw a painful inference— what is it?' he asked.

'What?' repeated Hugh, and added absently, 'who can tell?'

Up and down the room he walked restlessly, his eyes bent on the floor, his face drawn down into lines.   At length he stood and picked up the hat he had thrown on the couch.

'Bonnithorne,' he said, 'you and I thought we saw into the heart of a mystery. Heaven pity us for blind moles, I fear we saw nothing.'

' Why—what—how so—when——' the lawyer stammered with the conventional smile, and then stopped short.

Hugh had walked out of the room and out of the house.   He leapt into the saddle and rode away.

The wind had risen yet higher; it blew an icy blast from behind him as he cantered home.   Through the hazy atmosphere a cloud of dun vapourish red could be seen trailing over the dim fells.   It poised above the ball crown of the Eel Crag like a huge supernatural bird with outstretched wings.

Hugh held the reins with half-frozen hands. He barely felt the biting cold. His soul was in a tumult, and he was driven on by fears that were all but insupportable. For months a thick veil had overspread his conscience, and now in an instant, and by an accident, it was being rent asunder. He had lulled his soul to sleep. But no opiate of sophistry could keep the soul from waking. His soul was waking now. He began to suspect that he had been acting like a scoundrel.

At the Vicarage he stopped, dismounted, and entered. Standing in the hall, he overheard voices in the kitchen. They were those of Brother Peter and little Jacob Berry, the tailor, who had been hired to sew by the day, and was seated on the dresser.

'I've heeard of such sights afore,' the little tailor was saying. 'When auld Mother Langdale's son was killed at wrustlin' down Borrowdale way, and Mother Langdale was abed with the rheumatis, she saw him come to the bed-head a-dripping wet with blood, as plain as plain could be, and in less nor an hour after they brought him home to the auld body on a shutter—they did for sure.'

'Shaf on sec stories; I don't know as some folks aren't as daft as Mother Langdale hersel',' Peter muttered in reply.

Hugh Ritson beat the door heavily with his riding-whip.

'Parson Christian at home now?' he asked, when Peter opened it.

'Been and gone,' said Peter.

'Did you tell him I meant to come back?'

'Don't know as I did.'

Hugh's whip came down impatiently on his leggings.

'Do you know *anything?*' he asked. 'Do you know that you are now talking to a gentleman?'

'Don't know as I do,' mumbled Peter, backing in again.

'If Miss Greta is at home, tell her I should be glad to speak with her—do you hear?' Peter disappeared.

Hugh was left alone in the hall. He waited some minutes, thinking that Peter was carrying his message. Presently he overheard that worthy re-opening the discussion on Mother Langdale's sanity with little Jacob in the kitchen. The deep damnation he desired just then for Brother Peter was about to be indicated by another lusty rap on the kitchen door, when the door of the parlour opened, and Greta herself stood on the threshold with a smile and an outstretched hand.

'I thought it was your voice,' she said, and led the way in.

'Your cordial welcome heaps coals of fire on my head, Greta. I cannot forget in what spirit we last talked and parted.'

'Let us think no more about it,' said Greta, and she drew a chair for him to the fire.

He remained standing, and as if benumbed by strong feeling.

'I have come to speak of it — to ask pardon for it—I was in the wrong,' he said falteringly.

She did not respond, but sat down with drooping eyes. He paused, and there was an ominous silence.

'You don't know what I suffered or what I suffer still. You are very happy. I am a miserable man. Greta, do you know what it is to love without being beloved? How can you know? It is torture beyond the gift of words—misery beyond the relief of tears. It is not jealousy; that is

no more than a vulgar kind of envy. It is
a nameless, measureless torment.'

He paused again. She did not speak.
His voice grew tremulous.

' I'm not one of the fools who think that
the souls that are created for each other
must needs come together—that destiny
draws them from the uttermost parts of the
earth—that, trifle as they will with their
best hopes, fate is stronger than they are,
and truer to the pole-star of ultimate
happiness. I know the world too well to
believe nonsense like that. I know that
every day, every hour, men and women are
casting themselves away — men on the
wrong women, women on the wrong men
—and that all this is a tangle that will
never, never be undone.'

He stepped up to where she sat and
dropped his voice to a whisper.

' Greta—permit me to say it—I loved you
dearly. Would to heaven I had not. My

love was not of yesterday. It was you and
I, I and you. That was the only true
marriage possible to either of us from
world's end to world's end. But Paul
came between us ; and when I saw you
give yourself to the wrong man——'

Greta had risen to her feet.

'You say you come to ask pardon for
what you said, but you really come to
repeat it.' So saying she made a show
of leaving the room.

Hugh stood awhile in silence. Then he
threw off his faltering tone and drew himself up.

'I have come,' he said, 'to warn you
before it is too late. I have come to say,
while it is yet time, " Never marry my
brother, for as sure as God is above us,
you will repent it with unquenchable tears
if you do." '

Greta's eyes flashed with an expression
of disdain.

'No,' she said; 'you have come to threaten me—a sure sign that you yourself have some secret cause for fear.'

It was a home-thrust, and Hugh was hit.

'Greta, I repeat it, you are marrying the wrong man.'

'What right have you to say so?'

'The right of one who could part you for ever with a word.'

Greta was sore perplexed. Like a true woman, she would have given half her fortune at that moment to probe this mystery. But her indignation got the better of her curiosity.

'It is false,' she said.

'It is true,' he answered. 'I could speak the word that would part you wider than the poles asunder.'

'Then I challenge you to speak it,' she exclaimed.

They faced each other, pale and with quivering lips.

'It is not my purpose. I have warned you,' he said.

'You do not believe your own warning,' she answered.

He winced, but said not a word.

'You have come to me with an idle threat, and fear is written on your own face.'

He drew his breath sharply, and did not reply.

'Whatever it is, you do not believe it.'

He was making for the door. He came back a step.

'Shall I speak the word?' he said with a cold smile. 'Can you bear it?'

'Leave me,' she said, 'and carry your falsehood with you.'

He was gone in an instant. Then her anger cooled directly, and her woman's curiosity came back with a hundred-fold rebound.

'Gracious heaven, what did he mean?' she thought, and the hot flush mounted to her eyes. She had half a mind to call him back. 'Could it be true?' The tears were now rolling down her cheeks! 'He has a secret power over Paul—what is it?' She ran to the door. 'Hugh, Hugh.' He was gone. The galloping feet of his horse were heard faint in the distance. She went back into the house and sat down, and wept galling tears of pride and vexation.

CHAPTER VII.

At midday Parson Christian came home from the fields to dinner. 'I've been away loading turf,' he said, 'from Cole Moss, for Robin Atkinson, to pay him for loan of his gray mare on Saturday when I fetched my grain to the mill. Happen most of it is burnt up though,—but that's no fault of Robin's. So now we neither owe t'other anything, and we're straight from the beginning of the world.'

Greta was bustling about, with the very efficient hindrance of Brother Peter's assistance, to get the dinner on the table. She smiled, and sometimes tossed her fair head mighty jauntily, and laughed out loud with a touch of rattling gaiety. But there were rims of red around her bleared eyes, and her voice, beneath all its noisy merriment, had a tearful lilt.

The parson observed this, but said nothing about it. ' Coming round by Harrass End I met John Lowthwaite,' he said, ' and John would have me go into his house and return thanks for his wife's recovery from childbed. So I went in, and warmed me, and drank a pot of ale with them, and assisted the wife and family to return praise to God.'

Dinner was laid, little Jacob Berry came in from the kitchen, and all sat down together — Parson Christian and Greta, Brother Peter, and the tailor hired to sew.

' Dear me, I'm Jack-of-all trades, Greta, my lass,' said the parson after grace. 'Old Jonathan Truesdale came running after me at the bridge, to say that Mistress Truesdale wanted me to go and taste the medicine

that the doctor sent her from Keswick, and
see if it hadn't opium in it, because it made
her sleep. I sent word that I had business
to take me the other way, but would send
Miss Greta if she would go. Jonathan said
his missus would be very thankful, for she
was lonesome sometimes.'

'I'll go and welcome,' said Greta. The
rims about her eyes were growing deeper :
the parson chattered on to banish the
tempest of tears that he saw was coming.

'Well, Peter, and how did the brethren
at the meeting-house like the discourse yesterday afternoon ?'

'Don't know as they thought you were
varra soond on the point of 'lection,' muttered Peter from the inside of his bowl of
soup.

'Well, you're right homely folk down
there, and I'd have no fault to find if you
were not a little too disputatious. What's
the use of wrangling over doctrine ? Right

or wrong, it will matter very little to any
of us in a hundred years. We're on our
way to heaven, and, please God, there'll be
no doctrine there.'

Greta could not eat. She had no
appetite for food. Another appetite—the
appetite of curiosity—was eating at her
heart. She laid down her knife. The
parson could hide his concern no longer.
'Dear me, my lass, you and that braw lad
of yours are like David and Jonathan, and'
(with a stern wag of his white head) ' I'm
not so sure that I won't turn myself into
Saul, and fling my javelin at him for
envy.'

The parson certainly did not look too
revengeful at that moment, with the mist
gathering in his eyes.

'Talking of Saul,' said little Jacob,
' there's that story of the witch of En-dor,
and Saul seein' Sam'el when he was dead.
I reckon as that's no'but another version

of what happened at the fire a' Saturday
neet.'

Parson Christian glanced furtively at
Greta's drooping head, and then meeting the
tailor's eye, he put his finger to his lips.

When dinner was over the parson lifted
from the shelf the huge tome, 'made to
view his life and actions in.' He drew his
chair to the fire and began to turn over the
earliest leaves. Greta had thrown on her
cloak, and was fixing her hat.

'I'm going to see poor Mrs. Truesdale,'
she said. Then, coming behind the old
man, and glancing over his shoulder at the
book on his knees, 'What are you looking
for?' she asked, and smiled ; 'a prescription
for envy?'

The parson shook his old head gravely.
'You must know I met young Mr. Ritson
this morning.'

'Hugh?'

'Yes; he was riding home from his

iron pits, but stopped and asked me if I could tell him when his father, who is dead and gone, poor fellow, came first to these parts, and how old his brother Paul might be at that time.'

' Why did he ask ?' said Greta eagerly.

' Nay, I scarce can say. I told him I could not tell without looking at my book. Let me see ; it must be a matter of seven-and-twenty years ago. How old is your sweetheart, Greta ?'

' Paul is twenty-eight.'

' And this is the year seventy-five. Twenty-eight from seventy-five — that's forty-seven. Paul was a wee toddle, I remember. I'll look for forty - seven. Eighteen forty-four, forty-five, forty-six — here it is—forty-seven. And, bless me, the very page. Look, here we have it.'

Then the parson read this entry in his diary :

' " Nov. 18th.—Being promised to preach

at John Skerton's church at Ravenglass, I got ready to go thither. I took my mare and set forward and went direct to Thomas Storsacre's, where I was to lodge. It rained sore all the way, and I was wet, and took off my coat and let it run an hour. Then we supped and sat discoursing by the fire till near ten q'clock of one thing and another, and, among the rest, of one Allan Ritson, who has newly settled at Ravenglass. Thomas said Allan was fresh from Scotland, being Scottish born, and that his wife was Irish, and that they had a child, called Paul, only a few months old and not yet walking."

'The very thing! Wait, here's something more:

'"Nov. 19th (Lord's Day).—Went to church, and many people came to worship. Parson Skerton read the prayers and Thomas Storsacre the lessons. I prayed, and preached from Matt. vii. 23, 24; then ceased, and dismissed the people. After service, Thomas brought his new neighbour, Allan Ritson, who asked me to visit him that day and dine. So I went with him, and saw his wife and child—an infant in arms. Mrs. Ritson is a woman of some education and much piety. Her husband is a rough, blunt dalesman of the good old type."

'The very thing,' the parson repeated; and he put a mark in the page.

'I wonder why he wants it?' said Greta.

She left Parson Christian still looking at his book, and went out on her errand.

She was more than an hour gone, and when she returned the winter's day had all but closed in. Only a little yellow light still lingered in the sky.

'Greta, they have sent for you from the Ghyll,' said the parson as she entered. 'Mrs. Ritson wants to see you to-night. Natt, the stableman, came with the trap. But he has gone again.'

'I shall follow him at once,' said Greta.

'Nay, my lass, the day is not young enough,' said the parson.

'I was never afraid of the dark,' said Greta.

She took down a lantern and lit it, drew her cloak more closely about her, and prepared to go.

'Then take this paper to young Mr. Hugh. It's a copy of what is written in my book.'

Greta hesitated. But she could not tell Parson Christian what had passed between Hugh and herself. She took the paper and hastened away.

The parson sat for a while before the fire. Then he rose, walked to the door, and opened it. 'Heaven bless the girl, it's snowing. What a night for the child to be abroad!' He returned in disturbed humour to the fireside.

WHEN Greta set out, the atmosphere was yellow and vapourish. The sky grew rapidly darker. As she reached the village, thin flakes of snow began to fall. She could feel them driven by the wind against her face, and when she came by the inn she could see them in the dull yellow light.

The labourers were leaving the fields, and, with their breakfast cans swung on their fork handles, they were drifting in twos and threes into the Flying Horse. It looked warm and snug within.

She passed the little cluster of old houses, and scarcely saw them in the deepening night. As she went by the mill she could just descry its ruined roof standing out like a dark pyramid against the dun sky. The snow fell faster. It was now lying thick on her cloak in front, and on the windward face of the lantern in her hand.

The road was heavier than before, and she had still fully a quarter of a mile to go. She hastened on. Passing the little church—Parson Christian's church—she met Job Sheepshanks, the letter-cutter, coming out of the shed in the churchyard. 'Bad night for a young lady to be from home, begging your pardon, miss,' said Job, and went on towards the village, his bunch of chisels clanking over his shoulder.

The wind soughed in the leafless trees that grew around the old roofless barn at the corner of the road that led to the fells. The gurgle of a half-frozen waterfall came from the distant Ghyll. Save for these sounds and the dull thud of Greta's step on the snow-covered road, all around was still.

How fast the snow fell now. Yet Greta heeded it not at all. Her mind was busy with many thoughts. She was thinking of Paul as Parson Christian's great book had pictured him—Paul as a child, a little darling babe, not yet able to walk. Could it be possible that Paul, her Paul, had once been that? Of course, to think like this was foolishness. Every one must have been young at some time. Only it seemed so strange. It was a sort of mystery.

Then she thought of Paul the man—Paul as he had been, gay and heartsome ; Paul as he was, harassed by many cares. She thought of her love for him—of his love for her—of how they were soon, very soon, to join hands and face the unknown future in an unknown land. She had promised. Yes, and she would go.

She thought of Paul in London, and how soon he would be back in Newlands. This was Monday, and Paul had promised to come home on Wednesday. Only two days more ! Yet how long it would be after all !

Greta had reached the lonnin that went up to the Ghyll. She would soon be there. How thick the trees were in the lane ! They shut out the last glimmer of light from the sky. The lantern burned yellow amidst the snow that lay on it like a crust.

Then Greta thought of Mrs. Ritson. It was strange that Paul's mother had sent for her. They were friends, but there had never been much intimacy between them. Mrs. Ritson was a grave and earnest woman, a saintly soul, and Greta's lightsome spirit had always felt rebuked in her presence. Paul loved his mother, and she herself must needs love as well as reverence the mother of Paul. It was Paul first and Paul last. Paul was the centre of her world. She was a woman, and love was her whole existence.

Here in the lonnin she was in pitch darkness. She stumbled once into the dyke; then laughed and went on again. At one moment she thought she heard a noise not far away. She stood and listened. No, it was nothing. Only a hundred yards more! Bravely!

Then by a swift rebound—she knew not why—her mind went back to the events of the morning. She thought of Hugh Ritson and his mysterious threat. What did he mean? What harm could he do them? Oh that she had been calmer, and asked! Her heart fluttered. It flashed upon her that perhaps it was he and not his mother who had sent for her to-night. Her pulse quickened.

At that instant the curlew shot over her

head with its deep, mournful cry. At the same moment she heard a step approaching her. It came on quickly. She stopped. ' Who is it ?' she asked.

There was no answer. The sound of the footstep ceased.

' Who are you ?' she called again.

Then with heavy thuds in the darkness and on the snow, some one approached. She trembled from head to foot, but advanced a step and stopped again. The footstep was passing her. She brought the light of the lantern full on the retreating figure.

It was the figure of a man. Going by, hastily, he turned his head over his shoulder and she saw his face. It was the face of Paul—colourless—agitated—with flashing eyes.

Every drop of Greta's blood stood still.

' Paul !' she cried, thrilled and immovable.

There was an instant of unconsciousness.

The earth reeled beneath her. When she came to herself she was standing alone in the lane, the lantern half-buried in the snow at her feet.

Had it been all a dream?

She was but twenty yards from the house. The door of the porch stood open. Chilled with fear to the heart's core, she rushed in. No one in the hall. Not a sound, but the faint mutter of voices in the kitchen.

She ran through the passage, and threw open the kitchen door. The farm labourers were at supper, chatting, laughing, eating, smoking.

'Didn't you hear somebody in the house?' she cried.

The men got up and turned about. There was dead silence in a moment.

'When?'

'Now.'

'No. What body?'

She flew off without waiting to explain

The kitchen was too far away. Hugh Ritson's room opened from the first landing of the stairs. The stairs went up almost from the porch. Darting up, she threw open the door of Hugh's room. Hugh was sitting at the table, examining papers by a lamp.

'Have you seen Paul?' she cried, in an agonized whisper, and with a panic-stricken look.

Hugh dropped the papers, and rose stiffly to his feet.

'Great God, where?'

'Here—this instant.'

Their eyes met. He did not answer. He was very pale. Had she dreamed? She looked down at the snow-crusted lantern in her hand. It must have been all a dream.

She stepped back on to the landing, and stood in silence. The serving people had come out of the kitchen, and, huddled

together, they looked up at her in amazement. Then a low moan reached her ear.
She ran to Mrs. Ritson's room. The door
to it stood wide open ; a fire burned in the
grate, a candle on the table.

Outstretched on the floor lay the mother
of Paul, cold, still, and insensible.

When Mrs. Ritson regained consciousness she looked about with the empty gaze
of one who is bending bewildered eyes on
vacancy. Greta was kneeling beside her,
and she helped to lift her into the bed. She
did not speak. But she grasped Greta's
hand with a nervous twitch, when the girl
whispered something in her ear. From time
to time she trembled visibly, and glanced
with a startled look towards the door. But
not a word did she utter.

Thus hour after hour wore on, and the
night was growing apace. A terrible silence
brooded over the house. Only in the kitchen
was any voice raised above a whisper.

There the servants quaked and clucked—
every tongue among them let loose in con-
jecture and the accents of surprise.

Hugh Ritson passed again and again from
his own room to his mother's. He looked
down from time to time at the weary, pale,
and quiet face. But he said little. He put
no questions.

Greta sat beside the bed, only less weary,
only less pale and quiet, only less disturbed
by horrible imaginings than the sufferer
who lay upon it.

Towards midnight Hugh came to say that
Peter had been sent for her from the Vicarage.
Greta rose, put on her cloak and hat, kissed
the silent lips, and followed Hugh out of
the room.

As they passed down the stairs Greta
stopped at the door of Hugh Ritson's room,
and beckoned him to enter it with her.
They went in together, and she closed the
door.

'Now tell me,' she said, 'what this means.'

Hugh's face was very pale. His eyes had a wandering look, and when he spoke his voice was muffled. But by an effort of his unquenchable energy he shook off this show of concern, and smiled feebly.

'It means,' he said, 'that you have been the victim of a delusion.'

Greta's pale face flushed. 'And your mother—has she also been the victim of a delusion?'

Hugh shrugged his shoulders, showed his teeth slightly, but made no reply.

'Answer me—tell me the truth—be frank for once—tell me, can you explain this mystery?'

'If I could explain it, how would it be a mystery?'

Greta felt the blood tingle to her finger tips.

'Do you believe I have told you the truth?' she asked.

' I am sure you have.'

' Do you believe I saw Paul in the lane ?'

' I am sure you think you saw him.'

' Do you know for certain that he went away ?'

Hugh nodded his head.

' Are you sure he has not got back ?'

' Quite sure.'

' In short, you think what I saw was merely the result of woman's hysteria ?'

Hugh smiled through his livid lips, and his staring eyes assumed a momentary look of amused composure. He stepped to the table and fumbled some papers.

This reminded Greta of the paper the parson had asked her to deliver. ' I ought to have given you this before,' she said. ' Mr. Christian sent it.'

He took it without much apparent interest, put it on the table unread, and went to the door with Greta.

The trap was standing in the courtyard, with Natt in the driver's seat and Brother Peter in the seat behind. The snow had ceased to fall, but it lay several inches deep on the ground. There was the snow's dumb silence on the earth and in the air.

Hugh helped Greta to her place, and then lifted the lamp from the trap, and looked on the ground a few yards ahead of the horse. 'There are no footprints in the snow,' he said, with a poor pretence at a smile—'none, at least, that go from the house.'

Greta herself had begun to doubt. She lacked presence of mind to ask if there were any footprints at all except Peter's. The thing was done and gone. It all happened three hours ago, and it was easy to suspect the evidence of the senses.

Hugh returned the lamp to its loop. 'Did you scream,' he asked, ' when you saw —when you saw—*it ?*'

Greta was beginning to feel ashamed.

'I might have done. I cannot positively
say——'

'Ah, that explains everything. No doubt
mother heard you and was frightened. I
see it all now. Natt, drive on—cold journey—good-night.'

Greta felt her face burn in the darkness.
Before she had time or impulse to reply
they were rolling away towards home.

At intervals her keen ear caught the
sound of suppressed titters from the driver's
seat. Natt was chuckling to himself with
great apparent satisfaction. Since the fire
at the mill he had been putting two and
two together, and he was now perfectly con-
fident as to the accuracy of his computation.
When folk said that Paul had been at
the fire he laughed derisively, because he
knew that an hour before he had left him
at the station. But an idea works in a
brain like Natt's pretty much as the hop fer-
ments. When it goes to the bottom it leaves

froth and bubbles at the top. Natt knew
that there was some grave quarrel between
the brothers. He also knew that there were
two ways to the station and two ways back
to Newlands—one through the town, the
other under Latrigg. Mister Paul might
have his own reasons for pretending to go
to London, and also his own reasons for not
going. Natt had left him stepping into the
station at the town entrance. But what
was to prevent him from going out again at
the entrance from Latrigg? Of course that
was what he had done. And he had never
been out of the county. Deary me, how
blind folk were, to be sure! Thus Natt's
wise head chuckled and clucked.

At one moment Natt twisted this sapient
and facetious noddle over his shoulder to
where Brother Peter sat huddled into a
hump and in gloomy silence. 'Mercy me,
Peter,' he cried in an affrighted whisper
and with a mighty tragical start, 'and is

that thee? Dusta know I thowt it were thy ghost.'

'Don't know as it's not—dragging a body frae bed a cold neet like this,' mumbled Peter, numbed up to his tongue, but still warm enough there.

END OF VOL. I.

BILLING & SONS, PRINTERS, GUILDFORD.